TEACH YOU TO LOVE ME

B. CELESTE

Cover Design: Letitia Hasser, RBA Designs
Editing: Proofing Style by Marla

ALSO BY B. CELESTE

To my loyal Lindon U readers

PLAYLIST

"Beautiful Mess"—Diamond Rio
"Just A Kiss"—Lady A
"Come Over"—Sam Hunt
"Guilty as Sin"—Taylor Swift
"It'll Be Okay"—Shawn Mendes
"Slow Hands"—Niall Horan
"Wish You'd Miss Me"—Chase Wright
"If Our Love is Wrong"—Calum Scott
"The Good I'll Do"—Zach Bryan
"Dancing with a Stranger"—Sam Smith ft Normani

PROLOGUE

Matt

B REAKING AWAY FROM the bellowing laughter of my obnoxious teammates in the locker room, I jerk to a halt when I pass the office that's been empty since Dorothy, our former athletic adviser, retired. My lips curl up, seeing a lush ass bent over the desk that definitely doesn't belong to a seventy-year-old woman. I lean against the doorjamb and stare in appreciation.

"If you take a picture, it'll last longer," the mysterious woman says, her voice a featherlight touch that has my heart doing some funny rom-com shit I don't like.

She straightens to reveal a lean frame hugged by a white button-down and black pencil skirt. It's the most dressed-up anybody gets outside of game day here at Lindon University.

When she turns, I'm greeted with a pretty face that has me standing to my full six-two height. *Damn.* Whoever the petite brunette is can't be that much older than the twenty-somethings that most of us football players are.

"Is that an invitation?" I ask, my lopsided grin stretching wider.

My eyes roam from her long brown hair resting over her shoulders to the thick black glasses that somehow highlight her unamused eyes, all the way down to her slim legs exposed in the skirt that rests just below her knees.

When she peels those glasses off, it reminds me of the librarian porn I used to search back in high school. All that's missing is a plaid skirt and a ruler. Damn shame too.

She shifts on the thin black heels that make her a few inches taller, shoulders drawing back in cautious professionalism. "With a comment like that, you must be Ricky Wallace, Matthew Clearwater, or Daniel Bridges."

"Junior," I reply easily about the other wide receiver on Lindon's football team. "We call him DJ. And I'm not even going to entertain your offensive assumption that I'm Wallace. That dude is a fucking dick. He's gotten worse since our captain tore his ACL. Pearce is thinking about having him start, but even he's getting sick of his shit, and that says a lot."

Coach Pearce is a great coach with a horrible moral code, so scumbags like Ricky Wallace can get away with a lot more than he should because he can throw a football and score a touchdown. It's not right, but it's become part of the norm for all of us on the team.

The Anne Hathaway lookalike can't hide the twitch of amusement that nearly lifts her pink lips as she rounds the desk and takes a seat behind it. "I take it you're Matthew, then."

I walk in and extend my hand, noticing the pretty green-brown color of her eyes as she stares at my outreached arm. Hazel. Warm. Inviting.

"Matt. And since you have the inside scoop and the office, I'm going to assume you're the new athletic adviser that Pearce told us not to mess with. I'm starting to see why."

She takes my hand and shakes it once, her grip firm. No ring. No tan line. I like her even more. "Yet here you are, Mr. Clearwater."

Chuckling at her formality, I drop my hand and cross my arms over my chest. "Maybe I'm the team's welcoming committee, and it's my job to greet all the newcomers. Especially the pretty ones."

She hums and leans back in her chair. "I might have believed you if you brought me a goodie basket and delivered it without staring at my ass or flirting."

I have no doubt the firecracker sitting in front of me is going to fit in well here. "You're not what I thought you'd be. The last adviser we had was a crotchety old woman named Dorothy."

I'm definitely not complaining about the change of pace, and I doubt the others will mind, considering we're used to testosterone-filled jockstraps around here. Plus, Anne Hathaway was my first celebrity crush growing up.

Her lips curl upward softly. "I like the name Dorothy. It reminds me of my favorite movie growing up."

"What was that?"

"*The Wizard of Oz.*"

I make a face at the film choice. My family still won't let me live down the time I cried as a child when the flying monkeys came on the screen. To this day, I refuse to watch the movie because of it.

Choosing to hold on to my pride, I don't share that piece of information. "You didn't tell me your name."

Her smile remains professional. "Rachel, but *you* can call

me Ms. Holloway."

Before I can make another remark, I hear a grumbled, "Let's go, Clearwater."

Turning to see Aiden Griffith and Caleb Anders, the team's tight end and running back, I hold up my finger to signal another minute. "It was nice meeting you, Rach. I'll get right on that goodie basket so you feel properly welcomed to the sausage fest. I'm almost twenty-one, so we can also get a drink sometime to really get to know each—"

Griffith grabs my arm and pulls me out of the office, shoving me lightly in front of him so I can't keep talking to the new addition to the football staff. "Don't even think about it," the broody buzzkill with arms the size of my head tells me.

Caleb chuckles at the mumbled warning.

I look over my shoulder at the two of them and wink. "I don't know what you're talking about, Griff."

His eyes narrow, but I just keep smiling.

I blame his grumpiness on the lack of sex he's having. Since he all but started stalking the cute blue-haired girl at Bea's Bakery in town, his mood has been off. Maybe if he'd finally get some, he'd stop shitting on the rest of us for trying to have a little fun.

A guy can only dream.

The next day, I slip into the dark office at the ass-crack of dawn with a wicker basket of food and drinks that I put together myself. Okay, and with some help from my mother. Not that anyone needs to know that. I don't bother leaving a card because I know Rachel Holloway will know exactly who left it.

Later that day, when I'm exiting the locker room, I see her small smile as she paws through the odds and ends I put inside.

Victory swells my chest.

I've already started winning her over.

CHAPTER ONE

Rachel

S MOOTH, HARD SKIN greets the palm of my hand as I come to, with the sun beaming through the half-open shades. For a minute, I think nothing of it as my eyelids flutter open and fight the grogginess that beckons another ten minutes of sleep.

A dream, the half-asleep version of me decides. *It's just a dream.*

Because I've had them before. They usually start with a lot of heated touching and end with warm cuddles just like this. And each time I woke up with my heart racing and other parts of me throbbing, I realized that the star of the dream was the same every single time. Then, with a guilty consciousness, I would force myself back to sleep and pray Matthew Clearwater didn't reappear.

A dream, I tell myself again as I snuggle into the warmth cocooning me.

Then my fingertips graze over coarse hair, and the strange, warm mattress moves under me.

Eyes opening, I come face-to-face with a naked torso carved with lean muscle. Suddenly, my senses are over-whelmed by the familiar scent of Old Spice that wraps around me like the cotton sheets tangled between my legs.

Then I feel the subtle throb from one too many glasses of wine that I had last night. God. How many had I had?

A husky noise rises from Matthew Clearwater's throat as his chest rises and falls under my touch.

Oh my God.

I close my eyes and think, *Shit.*

Sitting up, the sheets pool around my waist, and a cool breeze pebbles my bare skin. When I glance down, a shooting pain echoes in my skull as I glance at my body.

Naked as the day I was born.

"Not a dream," I whisper, remembering bits and pieces from the night before. From the moment I hung up the phone on my father when he told me the latest updates on him and his new girlfriend, to Matthew inviting me out to Dante's Pizzeria with the guys for a post-game celebration, to the shameless flirting that made me feel so much lighter after the fight I'd gotten into with my dad. He made me laugh, smile, and stop thinking about the betrayal that boiled my blood.

…until he was the one boiling my blood for a lot of other reasons that had to do with that mouth he used to charm me over on numerous occasions.

My body thrums to life with the memory of all the ways he worked it after I told him *yes.*

"Not a dream," I say to myself again.

I reach for my phone resting on the nightstand and cringe when I see the time.

"Matt," I groan, clenching the sheets to my chest to cover myself as I use my free hand to shake the sleeping boy beside me. "Wake up."

An indiscernible noise comes from him as he turns onto his side, giving me his back.

More moments from last night resurface as I stare at the well-formed muscles he earned through all his training on and off the field.

There was a celebration after the Dragons won their first game against the Raiders. Pizza. Beer. Wings. And after we ditched the pizzeria, there was wine. Lots of wine. And thanks to my love for the sweet kind, the hangover feels ten times worse. It churns my stomach, making nausea rise up the back of my throat as I remember the way he pinned my body against the wall outside of Dante's and asked that question I should have said no to.

Do you want this as bad as I do?

I did. I really did. Because I was having fun and not giving an ounce of thought to the consequences or other feelings that had previously weighed on my mind. At that moment, it was the two of us—not a student and his athletic adviser, but a boy who liked a girl.

Stupid. I was so stupid last night.

Another wave of nausea hits me. Karma, I'm sure, for the student currently in bed beside me despite the strict rules against it.

Shaking him again, I say, "Come on, Matthew. You need to get up and go before my neighbors see you."

For the most part, the other neighbors keep to themselves. Except for the ornery older woman, Mrs. Flynn, who was widowed almost eight years ago. A permanent scowl is carved onto her face whenever she sees me, and I'd take it personally if I didn't see her look at the mailman the same way. God only knows what she'd say if she saw Matt doing a six-a.m. walk of shame when she's outside walking her chihuahua.

"Five more minutes," the attractive blond says, swatting my hand away.

It's been two months since I met the boy trying to curl in my blankets. Merely sixty days, and I already caved into his charming personality and flirty innuendos despite my better judgment.

Yesterday wasn't a good day for me. I was sad. Angry. Confused. But those excuses don't justify the choice I made, no matter how much Matt made me laugh or feel good. I was the older one, granted not by much, and knew better.

"No," I hedge. God, how did I get myself into this mess? "Come on, Matt. Please? This isn't good. In fact, this is really, really bad."

He makes another disgruntled noise like he doesn't get the seriousness of what occurred between us.

I move him again, trying to keep the contents in my stomach where they are. "You've got a team meeting to go over game footage, and we both know how Coach Pearce is when you're late."

This time, he groans in defeat and flops over onto his back, and I know I've got him. The head coach of Lindon's football team is a stoic middle-aged man. He's serious ninety-nine percent of the time, and the one percent he isn't is only a generous assumption I made for his personal life outside of the university. Because God help anybody he's married to who would have to deal with his moodiness. I could only hope he was better off school property.

One of his unique gray-blue eyes pops open to look at me. The color is beautiful, not that a guy like Matt enjoyed being told that. But his eyes and the rest of him *are* beautiful, if I'm being honest. In a masculine sort of way.

His time on the field and in the weight room contributed to every lean, carved muscle covering his body. Pair that with those bluish-gray eyes and his moppy blond hair, and I was bound to be a goner the second he unabashedly got caught staring at my butt.

I just thought my willpower was stronger than two shared bottles of wine and cheesy pickup lines that never would have worked on me if I were sober. At least, that's what I tell myself.

"It's not Coach Pearce I'm worried about," he says, looping an arm around my waist and pulling me under him in a smooth maneuver like he's done this a million times before. And he probably has. Just not with me. "Griff has had a larger stick up his ass than usual lately."

I put my hands on his shoulders and squeeze them once, hoping he'll move. "Be nice. He's your friend."

"He's a nosy Nancy," he grumbles under his breath, using one of his free hands to move pieces of hair behind my ear. The gentle caress sends warmth down my limbs, giving me pause. "The guys call him the team mom because he's always scolding one of us for something. I swear, ever since Ivy came into his life, he's been testier than normal. Why should we be punished because he's not getting his dick wet?"

Ignoring his crudeness, I pat his arm. "I think it's sweet that he cares enough to nag about things regardless of what his motive may be. Can you please move now?"

"Even if he's nagged me about my intentions with you?"

My smile slips, and the headache gets worse as it drums in my skull. "What has he said?"

"He told me not to be a playboy and put your job at risk," he says casually. "If he cares about anyone, it's you."

For him to tell Matt that, he must suspect something. "Matt…"

He shakes his head, those heart-stopping eyes piercing mine into not pushing him off me. "Don't." He stops me before I can point out the obvious. "Get out of that pretty little head of yours. He doesn't think anything has happened."

"Then why—"

"You've been around us long enough to know we all have reputations," he says. It's unapologetic. Matter of fact. "Most athletes do. The games, the adrenaline, the attention…it gets to our heads. It's gotten to mine more times than I can count."

Nibbling my bottom lip, I slowly nod.

In my short time with the boys, I've gotten insight I never had as an onlooker in the stands. I've heard all the gossip, all the fights, and all of the makeups that happen between them, their friends, and the people they're dating.

And I *have* heard that the boys on the team were popular with the ladies…and some guys. They're young and attractive, so I wasn't shocked to hear I was surrounded by a handful of players outside the field.

The fact I'm in this particular position speaks volumes to what Coach Pearce told me when I first started working with the Dragons. *"These boys are every stereotype you've ever heard about,"* he warns, walking me to the office I'll be taking over. *"I've already told them not to mess with you, but there's always going to be someone who pushes boundaries. Don't let them."*

It was the first time I'd met the man who looked like he stepped on a Lego moments before. I hadn't gotten a handshake or a hello. Just a monotone "follow me" and a head nod in the opposite direction as he walked away. He wasn't part of the hiring process; he just told HR to bring in someone who could do the job, which was basically keeping his players on track in their coursework so they wouldn't be punished.

I don't like even the possibility of knowing that any of the players suspect something is going on between Matt and me because chances are that will get back to their coach. And even though I've heard the whispers surrounding what Coach Pearce has let slide in his many years as the head coach at the university, I'm not sure if he'd let somebody else crossing lines do the same.

And, frankly, I don't want to find out.

"You're overthinking," he accuses lightly, his fingertips dancing along the edge of my jawline.

"I'm justified," I argue, ignoring the faint tingles that his fingertips leave behind the path he traces over my skin.

"It's nothing."

"*This,*" I say, lightly pushing him up and off of me so I can sit up, "is not nothing. This can get me in big trouble if somebody finds out."

Matt sighs. "It was one time, Rach. I told you last night nobody would find out."

"But can you really make that promise?" I doubt with a frown weighing the corners of my lips down. "I enjoyed our time together. But…"

Well, the truth is, I like my job more. The independent study gives me credit and a paycheck, which is a win-win since my financial aid doesn't cover the apartment I live in, and I'd barely make ends meet otherwise.

A shadow masks the playful edge Matthew always has on his face, and I know I've put it there. But what did he expect? I may not be that much older than the twenty-one-year-old, but my position as Lindon faculty means that we're testing waters. And I've never been that strong of a swimmer.

His legs swing over the side of the bed, the sheets dropping to reveal a firm, toned backside that I have to force myself to look away from as he pulls his boxers on. "I'm glad you 'enjoyed your time.' Leave me a review on Yelp so more customers can come," he grumbles.

I cringe at his bitter tone. "You know that's not how I meant it."

Matt shakes his head as he dresses. "One of these days, you're going to throw caution to the wind and stop being afraid to live, Rach."

My nostrils flare with subtle irritation. "Says the boy who wouldn't lose everything if we get caught," I counter defensively. "Be honest, Matt. If people find out we slept together, you'll get high fives and congratulations, while I'll get a pink slip and be blacklisted from every school and university in the state. It's not the same for us."

He looks over his shoulder. "It's not like I'm underage."

"No," I agree. *Thank God.* "But you're a student, and

I'm a faculty member. There are rules in the handbook against those kinds of relationships because of HR nightmares that have happened in the past at Lindon. Everybody who gets hired is told to act professionally."

A slow, mischievous smirk curls half of Matt's lips. "I don't know. You were very courteous in ensuring I was given plenty of help last night. Can't get more professional than that."

I should have known he'd make a joke. "Now is not the time for humor."

His smirk drops after a few seconds when he sees the scowl I shoot him. "You're serious."

"Of course I am!" How could I not be? If he doesn't see what a risk this is, what am I even doing with him?

Hastily, I get out of bed with the sheets wrapped carefully around my body. It isn't like he didn't get a full view last night, but I'm not in the mood to be ogled right now.

"Come on, Rach—"

His words are cut off by the bathroom door that I close after grabbing a change of clothes.

I look at myself in the mirror, cringing when I see a red mark above my right breast. Teeth marks. Last night definitely got a little out of hand when everybody started breaking away in pairs when Dante's closed. Which is how Matt and I wound up with two bottles of wine that I definitely did not have already in my apartment, all but breaking down the door half-drunk with our mouths on each other before the lock could click into place.

Do you want this as bad as I do?

Touching the red mark, I internally sigh.

Why didn't I lie?

Knuckles wrap against the door as I'm half dressed, glad that I don't have any low necklines that could reveal where Matt's mouth was.

"I'm sorry," he says, his voice soft and genuine. "I didn't mean to sound like a prick."

Matt is a lot of things, but an asshole isn't one of them. Immature at times, sure. But not mean.

"I know," I tell him, pulling on the last piece of clothing and not bothering to study my messy just-had-sex hair in the mirror before running a brush through it.

My hand hesitates on the door handle before dropping it back down to my side.

"You should really go before someone sees you," I press, not wanting him to make up more excuses as to why he should stay.

There's silence on the other side of the wood, but I know he's still there.

Clearing my throat, I back up and sit on the closed toilet lid. "You don't want to be late," I remind him. "Coach Pearce threatened to bench you last time you showed after everybody else."

I think I hear him mumbling under his breath, but I don't catch what he says.

It feels like a long, tense few minutes when I finally hear him speak. "I'll see you at school then. And I'm...I'm sorry again."

Wetting my lips, I nod as if he can see me and stay silent. Words cram into the back of my throat as I wait and listen to him leave. It takes about five minutes before the door opens and closes, and I'm met with silence. Then I wait another five to make sure he actually left.

When I open the door, I'm by myself.

I look at the messy, unmade bed. Then at the clothes from last night scattered in a path from the door to the bedroom.

Swallowing, I toss the empty bottles of booze and start cleaning as if nothing ever happened.

My hand touches the red spot left behind again, knowing that's easier said than done.

CHAPTER TWO

Rachel

THE SPORTS COMPLEX looks like most of the other brick buildings on Lindon's campus, except for the gigantic red dragon painted onto the side by a few students from the art department, and the large lit-up signs pointing toward the football field entrance that the school invested in when ticket sales for games went up.

It was blatantly obvious when I moved here from Devon, a suburb of Philadelphia, that the town took their football seriously. I never understood the love for the sport until a few girls I roomed with my freshman year took me to the home games held on Friday nights. I was hooked by the addicting atmosphere of the crowd whenever the Dragons would get the ball and run with it seamlessly to the end zone.

I never expected that love to grow into an independent study with the football team until my professor, Dr. DuBois, offered me an opportunity after seeing the knowledge I held for the game. I'd gotten into a passionate, although some would argue heated, disagreement during one of his classes on athletic communications with a peer about the school's stats over the past three years and how the current team had a better chance at getting drafted into the pro league over any other Dragon in the past. When the elderly professor told me to stay behind, I thought I was going to get into trouble for the slightly aggressive conversation. Instead, he offered me an opportunity to put my skills to good use and help the current players make it to their full potential.

I got instant gratification that I may or may not have rubbed into Palmer's, my classmate, face. So I agreed.

"Kick slide, Chambers. Kick slide," I hear Coach Pearce yell loudly from the tunnel leading into the stadium.

Walking toward the coach's voice, I stop and study the field where the team is split in a T formation. Ever since accepting this position, it's given me an inside look that I've never gotten before. It makes me wonder if this is how my father felt when my late mother bought him sideline tickets to see the Eagles, his favorite football team.

The thought of them hurts. Because no matter how much I used to bond with my father over college and pro football, it doesn't excuse what he's done since Mom passed away from Huntington's disease only a short eight months ago. Losing her felt like losing a limb. And losing my father…it was a lingering phantom pain. There, but not.

Pearce blows the whistle around his neck and waves his clipboard in the air. "That would have gotten you flagged, Wallace. Anyone want to tell him why?"

It's number eleven who calls out, "Illegal blocking, Coach."

Matthew Clearwater.

My body tingles with the memories I've tried my hardest to push away for the past week. But every time I close my eyes, I swear I can feel his body hovering over mine, the slick sweat under my palms as I touch every inch of him, and the blissful release that took over me when his mouth worked the nerves between my thighs before feeling him slide inch by inch inside of me.

Stop, my conscious snaps.

I roll my shoulders and block out the pornographic re-plays happening in my mind.

"Go again," Pearce tells them. "And don't fuck it up this time, Wallace."

From a distance, I see Ricky Wallace lift a finger in the coach's direction. And it's not his index. He's lucky Pearce was looking at the clipboard, or he would have gotten benched.

They get back into formation, but my eyes are on one person only. When the ball snaps back, Ricky Wallace, the quarterback filling in following Justin Brady's ACL injury, runs with it until the left tackle gains on him. Wallace tosses the ball to Matthew, who catches it effortlessly and runs faster than anybody can catch him.

Five yards.

Ten.

Twenty.

Holy shit. Nobody gets close to him as he runs to the end zone, dropping the ball and moving his hips with number eighty-one—Daniel Bridges.

Junior.

Shaking my head at the dance Matthew and Daniel have clearly done plenty of times in celebration, I turn on my heel and head back to my office to get a few things done. Before I disappear into the tunnel, I feel a pair of eyes on me from the other side of the field.

It's not Matthew who's looking.

It's Aiden Griffith.

I force a smile, lifting my hand to give him a wave. His head dips in a singular nod, but that's it. It's only after he turns away that I feel my feet unglue from the ground so I can walk away.

I decide to focus on pulling grades for a few of the team members I haven't had check-ins with lately instead of thinking about what Aiden may or may not know.

I'm hunched over my laptop and jotting down notes on the infamous Ricky Wallace, whom I've heard very few good things about, when there's a knock on my door an hour and a half later.

Glancing up at the freshly showered wide receiver at my door, who resembles my mother's favorite country singer, Dierks Bentley, I offer him a smile. "Hi, Mr. Clearwater. What can I do for you?"

He walks in and sits down. I've studied his file enough to know that the six-foot-two football player is two hundred and twenty pounds of lean muscle with a borderline B average at Lindon. And after last week, I could confirm that was still true despite those stats being submitted two years ago during his sophomore year.

"It's Matt," he reminds me nonchalantly. "I'm way too young to be called mister anything; you should know that by now."

"Should I?" I question pointedly, eyebrows arched to remind him where we are. Familiarity doesn't belong in my very public office.

"I'm just pointing out that you age yourself by calling me

anything other than my first name," he says with a lift of his shoulders.

"I'd hardly say I'm old," is my only reply, eye twitching over the fact that I'm five years older than the boy occupying the seat across from me.

"You never told me how old you are," he realizes, studying me. "Why is that?"

"Didn't your mother teach you that it's rude to ask a woman her age?"

Matt snickers. "She did. She also told me never to ask a woman how far along she is. Forgot about that one and nearly got a yardstick to the face in eighth grade Spanish because I thought Mrs. Hubberman was pregnant."

Internally, I flinch. The poor woman.

"Speaking of Spanish," I tell him to diverge the conversation. "Your grade in Spanish One is low. You've only got a few months to fix it before it tanks your overall GPA."

"That means I still have a couple of months to get it up. Speaking of which—"

"Nope," I cut him off before he finishes whatever dirty thought he's thinking. I know him by now. He gets a gleam in his eyes when he's about to say something sarcastic. "Just make sure you study, okay? It's going to be easier to raise your grade now versus rushing to do it at the end of the term."

He salutes me. "Anything for you, Rach."

"Ms. Holloway," I correct.

"You're too young for that."

"Do you flirt with everyone?" I question, one I've asked him a number of times.

"I didn't flirt with Dorothy," he remarks with a smirk. "If I'd tried to, she probably would have castrated me."

I didn't know the woman, but I can believe it. With a name like that, I bet she had a feisty personality.

Shaking my head at his antics, I drop my pen and turn my computer screen away from his line of sight so he doesn't see the file on the second-string quarterback he's got beef with.

"I have work to finish," I tell him.

"Didn't your mom tell you it's impolite to ignore guests when they visit you?" he quips.

Without thinking, I say, "Maybe she would have taught me that if she were still alive."

Matthew frowns, making me feel bad for dropping that tidbit of information so coolly. But I'm tired. I feel guilty. And I'm confused.

None of those help my filter.

I murmur, "Sorry."

His slick grin is officially gone. "Shit, Rach...el. I'm sorry to hear that. Do you mind if I ask how she...?"

Wetting my lips, I instantly regret saying anything at all because having to talk about this isn't easy for me. "She was sick."

It's all I'm willing to offer. Watching Mom deteriorate from the neurological disorder was bad enough; I don't need to relive how it made her an entirely different person once it took over her independence.

The woman who used to love life could barely live it months before the end. Gone were the sunny days hiking together at the state park or training for the marathon we were planning to do together. Holidays spent baking and cooking in the kitchen were gone because she could barely eat. Torturing her with old family recipes seemed inhumane.

I hated what Huntington's did to the woman who was one of the most caring people I've ever known.

Matthew's expression dims, his lips twitching downward in sympathy. Something flashes in his eyes that goes beyond the typical pity I usually see when people hear about my mother's early death, but I don't know what he's thinking.

"Nobody should be without their mother," is the only thing he says, his voice quieter than normal.

I'm inclined to agree, but talking about it is impossible when I feel my throat thicken. The burn of impending tears prickles the back of my eyes, so I battle them off and straighten in my seat. "You aren't the only one with classes to pass, so if you don't mind..."

"Ahh. I forgot, Ms. Grad Student. You know, I've always appreciated older women."

"Like Dorothy?" I ask dryly.

He swipes at his mouth to hide the wavering smile. "Sure, Ruby Red. Like Dorothy."

Ruby Red? Like *The Wizard of Oz*.

Instead of entertaining this conversation any further, I ask, "Is there anything I can do for you today?"

Leaning forward in the chair and resting his elbows on his bent knees, he watches me for a solid minute before eventually standing and shaking his head. "Nothing you can help me with right now, Ms. Holloway. Maybe next time."

My eyes narrow at his suspicious tone.

"By the way," he says, stopping at the door and glancing

at me. "What did you think of my little end zone dance? I saw you watching."

Maybe I should be embarrassed that he caught me, but it wasn't like I was ogling him. I was impressed, something his ego clearly doesn't need to hear.

I pick up my pen. "I think you should keep your day job."

Snickering at my sarcasm, he hefts a heavy sigh. "Damn. If pro ball didn't work out, I was planning on joining the *Magic Mike* dance crew out in Vegas."

Rolling my eyes, I wave him off. "Have a good rest of your day," I say dismissively.

"You better come to our game tomorrow," he calls as he backs toward the doorway. "We're going to kick Morrison's ass."

"I have no doubt," I answer honestly. The Dragons are a strong team with a good chance of not only making it to the championships but winning it all.

His grin returns at the compliment.

"Matt," I say before he can walk out.

He cocks his head.

"We can't do that again," I say quietly, looking at the empty hallway behind him. "I'm trying to build something for myself that I can be proud of. That...my mother could be proud of me for."

The wide receiver is quiet for a long moment.

Then he nods. "I get it, Rach."

I swallow, grateful. "Friends?"

His lips twitch. "I have a lot of friends," he states, scratching the column of his throat. "But I guess one more wouldn't hurt."

I can tell he's disappointed, but there's no other way to do this. One night together is all there can be. It's all I have to offer.

"Friends," I repeat with a wavery smile.

He glances at the floor. "Come to the game," he says again, smiling at me when he lifts his head even though it doesn't entirely meet those gunmetal eyes. "To support the team. And your friend."

I rub my lips together. He's trying. So the least I can do is try too. "We'll see."

He watches me for a moment longer before turning on his heel and tapping the doorjamb before leaving me to my solitude.

That night, I stay home with a pint of ice cream I spent way too much money on at the gas station and watch trash TV with my little sister on the phone to talk about it.

The Dragons lose their game.

MATT AND DANIEL are horsing around in my office a month later as I gather paperwork for them to submit to their academic advisers when Aiden walks in and smacks them both upside the head. The tight end drops onto the small sofa off to the side that I found on sale at a thrift shop a week ago. I bribed a couple of the players with pizza to carry it inside and help me reorganize my office. Matt told me it's "what friends do for each other" with a subtle wink that I'm grateful Caleb Anders didn't catch when his back was turned.

"Quit it," Aiden tells the boys with a single look. "Rach doesn't need your bullshit today."

"Thanks, Aiden," I say, passing the boys two separate pieces of paper. "But I'm used to it by now."

Daniel looks around Matt at Aiden. "Yeah, lighten up. Not even Cap is this uptight about having a little fun."

Aiden deadpans, "That's because Brady is more focused on getting into med school than dealing with your dumb asses all the time."

He's not wrong. Every time I meet with the injured quarterback, he's always telling me about the schools he's applied to for when he graduates from here. Out of everyone on the team, he's got the most ambition outside of the grumpy tight end sprawled across my couch. "Matthew, you're all set. Pick up that Spanish grade if you want to keep playing. Got it?"

"Yes, ma'am," he says with a smirk, standing up and shoving Daniel one last time before looking back at me. "And you should reconsider that one-on-one tutoring. I'd love all the help I can get."

Despite myself, I can feel my face growing warm from the obnoxious flirting that he's obviously doing for a reaction from his friends. Daniel gives him a high five with a stretched grin on his face that Aiden rolls his eyes over.

Clearing my throat, I smile plainly. "I can certainly make you an appointment at the Student Center's tutoring department if that's what you feel you need."

Matt chuckles at my smooth reply. "I'll see you around, *Ms. Holloway.*"

He smacks a laughing Daniel on the shoulder before

leaving the room without a second look in either Aiden's or my direction.

Aiden moves over to the seat Matt was in and fist bumps Daniel, who turns to the tight end and asks, "I haven't seen any bags of dog shit lit on fire on our front step, so should I assume you made up with Ivy?"

I perk up with interest. "Aiden, did you get a girlfriend?"

I've heard the name get brought up a handful of times at practice, and once from the boy who sauntered out of here with unabashed confidence, but I don't plan on admitting that.

Daniel laughs. "That's classic, Rach. This guy? He barely even lets the jersey chasers near him, even when they're throwing themselves his way. More for us though."

I think that's sweet. "Some people want more than that, Daniel."

The wide receiver makes a face at me like I told him some people like throwing puppies off overpasses. "Aw, c'mon. You know I hate when you call me that."

I cross my arms on the edge of the desk and give *Daniel* an amused look. "That is your name, isn't it?"

He grumbles under his breath.

Aiden leans back, propping an arm up on the back of Daniel's chair. "Could be worse, Danny Boy. And who are you to talk anyway? You've been drooling over a chick who barely gives you the time of day."

Daniel glowers, and Aiden cracks the smallest grin at the information I didn't know and don't want to pry on. "Don't start."

I shake my head at them. "Well, I think it's nice if you

found a girl who isn't going to throw herself at you, Aiden."

That pulls Daniel out of his stupor. "If anything, he'll wind up on a case of *20/20* because of this chick. She's awesome, but intense as hell."

She sounds guarded, which I can relate to.

"Coach said you wanted to see me," Aiden redirects, looking at me instead of entertaining the conversation his friend wants to have.

Daniel rolls his eyes and looks at me too. "I can go now, right? Pass classes or else blah blah blah. I feel you. I'm hungry."

"When are you not?" Aiden asks.

He shrugs. "I'm a growing boy, Griff. I need the proper nutrients to dominate on the field." When his sly eyes refocus on me, I already know his next line is going to make me groan by the suggestive wiggle of his eyebrows. "And off the field."

Daniel reminds me of the golden retriever I had growing up—goofy and energetic. "You're free to go. You know what we talked about."

One more fist bump later, it's just me and Aiden left in my office. The first thing he says gives me pause. "Matt is persistent, you know. He doesn't give up easily when he puts his mind to it."

My eyes go from the file in front of me to him, my heart picking up in my chest at the implication. "I'm not sure I know what you mean, Aiden."

He watches me for a long moment before shaking his head and dropping it. I can tell there's something he wants to say, but he must decide it's not his place. "My grades have been good this semester, so I'm not sure why I'm here. Pearce mentioned a check-in."

I take a deep breath to collect myself and smile at him. It's forced at best, and all I can hope is that I don't look like the Joker. "It's mandatory to meet up a few times a semester to make sure everything is okay. Pearce asked me to talk to you about next year since you were invited to the combine." I open the file folder and scan the page. "Your stats this year have been stellar, and your grades are perfect. You want to be drafted, right?"

When I meet his eyes, he offers me another head dip of confirmation. "Coach says the combine will open that door for me. He suggested ending after this semester."

"Is that what you want? You're on top of your courses and in the top three of your class. It'd be a shame to see you stop right before getting your degree."

"It's just a piece of paper," is his reply. "I've never cared about college that much. It was only about football for me. Why stay if I get a shot at doing what I actually love?"

I nod in understanding, even if I'm tempted to encourage him to finish his degree first. He's so close to being done, with only one semester left. I suppose he could take a leave of absence and come back later, but it's rare that actually happens.

"I saw what ESPN was saying about you after your last game," I note, tapping my pen against my notepad. Despite the invitations I get from Matt and a few other Dragons, I don't always attend the games. I congratulate them on their wins and apologize for their losses whenever I see them next. But when curiosity gets the better of me, I find myself logging online to watch the live games in my apartment to keep a healthy distance while still cheering them on. It's the best I can do while keeping boundaries untouched. Or as untouched as they can be. "They seem optimistic that you'll be a first pick."

Aiden lifts a shoulder like that isn't new news.

It's clear he's not going to say anything, so I change my approach. "What about this girl you're supposedly into? Coach Pearce seems to think you're one of the few he can invest the most time in because you're never distracted by the wiles of college. Is she going to change that?"

His lips twitch. "Clearly, experiencing college like a normal guy didn't work out so well for me when I tried it the first time. I was booted and brought here, which is why Coach is so willing to invest his effort. He knows I won't fuck it up again. Not even for—" He doesn't say Ivy's name, making my brows go up slowly.

"This is about Wilson Reed," I conclude, realizing the tension in his shoulders doesn't have anything to do with a girl.

I know the story. His transfer from his first college is listed in the file I got on him. But it didn't seem like that situation was really his fault, even if he seems to shoulder a majority of the blame. "I fucked up and refuse to repeat the same mistakes. The girl…She won't be a problem."

I lift my hands. "I never said she would be. And we both know that Bill, Coach Pearce, wants what's best for you."

"He wants what's best for the team," he corrects dryly. "And so do I."

I've noticed his dedication to the sport the most out of

everybody I've met. His love for football pours from him. He's meant to play the game. But I hope he doesn't lose sight of everything else life has to offer because of it.

"Aiden, you do understand that it's okay to have more than football in your life, right? There's more than playing the game. Dating, especially at your age, is perfectly natural. It won't mess you up as long as it's a healthy relationship."

I'm met with silence. And maybe I'm pushing things too far. After all, I'm not here to be his therapist. I'm here to make sure he's passing. Clearly, I don't have stellar decision-making skills, considering the people I've allowed myself to get close to.

So, I let it go. "It looks like Wilson Reed will be one of your competitors at the end of the season with how you're both playing."

"So?"

"You didn't come here on the greatest terms. It may be hard to see some of your old teammates. I know a few of them graduated—"

He grips the armrests. "Can we just tell Coach we had this talk? I don't need a therapy session. No offense, but I have better stuff to do with my time than gossip about my old college or personal life."

Closing the folder when I hear his tone, I put it on the pile with a few others. "I only want to help, but if that's all you want to say today, then head out. I know you're busy."

Rubbing his lips together, he grabs his bag from the floor and hauls it over his shoulder. "I didn't mean to be a dick," he murmurs. It's not entirely apologetic, but I accept it like it is.

"You weren't. I get it."

"And about Matt…" He pauses, shifting on his feet. "He doesn't always think about others when he goes after things. Keep that in mind. You both have a lot to lose."

There's a long pause between us before I nod once and force a tight smile. I already know that, but the reminder is another reason why I made the choice I did. "Thank you, Aiden. Have a good day."

He looks at me for a moment longer before dipping his head one last time and making his exit.

Only when he leaves do I close my eyes and exhale a heavy breath.

CHAPTER THREE

Matt

R ESTING FIVE MINUTES outside the Lindon town line is the same blue and white farmhouse my parents moved into when they got married thirty years ago. Walking up the paved pathway reminds me of all my favorite things growing up—playing catch with my father, climbing the maple tree in the front yard, and helping my mother garden.

None of the other places I've lived compared to the house I've always called home. Not even the football house I share with the smelly assholes I play on the field with.

A small smile curls my lips as I open the front door, walking toward the smell of something sweet in the air that I know is coming from the kitchen.

"There he is," Mom greets, putting the cookie tray down on the counter and peeling the oven mitt off. "Perfect timing. I need a taste tester."

I chuckle as I round the counter and give her a hug and a kiss on the cheek. "The last thing I need is more sugar," I tell her, studying the chocolate chip cookies spread out. "Caleb has been baking for Raine at the house and giving us the leftovers. I've eaten my weight in brownies and pie."

Her eyebrows go up skeptically. "They better not be special brownies."

Groaning, I drop my head back. "That was *one* time, and Mav didn't even tell me they had anything in them." The experience in high school was traumatizing for me. I was paranoid the entire night after eating half a tray of pot brownies without realizing what was in them. "Plus, we get drug tested at random. The last thing I want is to have something in my system and lose my scholarship."

She pats my arm. "Good. One time was enough. Your father was so mad when he picked you up from that party..."

Not wanting to think about the night I got stoned and begged my dad to drive me to Taco Bell, only to throw up my crunch wrap five minutes later, I change the topic. "Are you doing another bake sale for the church or something?"

The woman with silver speckled into her dark hair turns and puts a few cookies from a different counter onto a paper plate for me. "I told Peggy that I'd help the booster club with their bake sale this year, although I don't know why. The woman drives me mad. Did I tell you she complained about the petunias I planted at the library last year? It isn't my fault there was a late frost that killed half of them."

Before I can reply to her rant, she passes the paper plate to me. "Anyway, I made ones with peanut M&M's since they're your favorite. You're too skinny. All that football is making you disappear."

Practice was hot and brutal today. The last thing I want is to load up on sugar, but when Mom gestures toward one of the chairs by the kitchen table and goes to the refrigerator to get me a glass of milk, I sit and watch her prepare a snack like she's done since I was little.

"I'm in the best shape of my life," I counter, patting my toned stomach. I love seeing the ab definition, but she might as well think it's my ribs popping out.

She harrumphs in disagreement. "Has practice gotten better with the new quarterback?"

The mention of Wallace has me scowling as she sets the cookies and milk in front of me. "No. I don't know why the kid thinks he's hot shit. We've all tried talking to him about it, but he thinks he's the best we've got, and Pearce isn't exactly doing anything to make him think otherwise."

She frowns. "Sounds like he needs to be knocked down a few pegs."

"Or ten," I grumble, breaking a cookie apart and shoving half of it into my mouth. Moaning from the sweetness exploding on my tongue, I give her an appreciative nod. "So good. DJ is going to be pissed he didn't tag along this time."

Mom laughs, busying herself by putting some of the cookies into plastic containers. "He's welcome anytime he wants. Same with the others. Maybe your quarter-back…What's his name?"

"Ricky Wallace."

She nods. "Maybe Ricky just needs a good home-cooked meal. You never know what people are going through in their personal lives. Sometimes, it takes killing someone with kindness to break through a few layers."

I think about Rachel's mother. I never would have known she lost somebody if she hadn't said it. As much as I wanted to know more, I could tell she was shutting down. Friends push, but even better friends know their boundaries.

Brushing her off, I focus on Wallace. "I don't think your

cookies are going to make him have a come to Jesus moment, Ma."

She shrugs. "You never know. These cookies did win at the local bake-off years ago."

I don't have the heart to tell her it's because there were only three other entries, and one of the judges found hair in her competitor's dessert, and the other competitor's cookies were undercooked.

"I guess we all were sort of like Wallace when we first got on the team. Griff told me once that Wallace reminded him of me." I flipped him off when he said that.

"God help your poor coach then," Mom muses with a shake of her head. "You and those boys have always been a handful. I couldn't imagine dealing with more of you."

I grin at the five-foot-two woman full of savagery. "We're lovable though."

She hums in amusement. "Lovable pains in the asses."

Snorting, I take another bite of the cookie and let the sugar soak into my tastebuds. "You wouldn't have it any other way. Your life would be boring without me in it. Admit it."

"Don't talk with food in your mouth," she chides, swatting me with the oven mitt. Her smile reappears. "But you're right. It would be. Your father and I were talking about it earlier."

"All good things, I hope."

"Just how strange it is to be empty nesters," she comments with a sigh. "You know how badly we wanted this house to be full of children. Now that it's just us…"

It's hard for them. I know they'd tried having their own

kids before opting for adoption, but I understood why they settled for only me. They'd done foster care a few times, and some of the kids they were assigned caused them more stress than they'd anticipated. I think they lost the energy to try adopting another kid because of the lengthy process it was just getting me and becoming fosters for other children who needed a temporary home. "It's not like I'm never around. I think you cook more for me now than you did when I lived here."

Mom hums thoughtfully. "That's because you can't survive off of microwavable meals and takeout for the rest of your life. You're going to give yourself high cholesterol. Do you know how much sodium is in some of those TV dinners?"

A lot probably. "That's what makes them taste so good," I reply easily. "And we take turns cooking at the house. Sometimes." I pause. "Okay, maybe Caleb cooks the most since he's actually decent at it. And now that Ivy is there, she's been pitching in. Except she served us burnt mac and cheese once, and I had to choke it down."

She eyes me. "That's exactly why I need to make sure you're eating properly. You don't want to be like your father with all his health problems, do you?"

Genetically, it's not like I could have the same issues he does, but I don't bother pointing that out. "Where *is* Dad?"

Once one container of cooled cookies is full, she grabs another one. "He told Larry he'd help cut some trees down that fell during the last storm. Did he tell you about the new chainsaw he got at Anders Hardware? Caleb's father gave him a deal on it, and I swear the man hasn't stopped playing with that thing since he brought it home. It's like when you bought him the edger for Father's Day last year. He offered to do all the neighbors' lawns just to use it."

He sent me a grainy photo of the chainsaw in question the other day. Part of his finger was in the frame, but I saw enough of the new toy to tell him it was nice. "You know you like it when he's out doing man shit with the neighbors. Remember last winter when he was bugging you every two seconds because he was bored?"

Mom laughs lightly, glancing up at me with soft blue eyes. "I knew he was going to go stir crazy once he retired from the town. I'm glad he's done with that because they were working him too hard in the garage. His poor back wasn't going to take it for much longer working on those plow trucks. But I swear if that man tells me he's bored one more time…"

Chuckling, I stuff another piece of the cookie into my mouth and watch her put the others away. "Send him my way if he gets on your nerves. I've got things around the house I need fixed. Caleb said he'd do it, and Griff said he'd call the landlord, but it never gets done."

Mom makes a face. "I still think you should move back home. I love some of those boys, but the others…"

She's never liked how rowdy we can be. It doesn't help that she's heard of the parties getting reported and broken up on more than one occasion since she goes to church with the local sheriff. "You just want me home to fatten me up and distract Dad," I tease lightheartedly.

"Now that I think about it…" She winks at me. "It's always nice to have you home, sweetie. But yes. I have selfish reasons. Being an empty nester isn't for everyone. I keep telling your father we should get a dog, but he thinks it'll get in the way of us traveling."

My brows pinch at that. "Since when do you two travel anywhere?"

She offers me a deadpan expression. "My point exactly. The man will make a million excuses about why he can't sit still, but he doesn't want a dog because it'll be too much work in case we decide to travel like we've talked about in the past. Make that one make sense."

Snorting, I finish off the first cookie she gave me and lean my arms on the edge of the table. "I'll watch your nonexistent puppy anytime you guys want to go away together. You deserve a long vacation. A little relaxation will be good for Dad's back."

Mom hums in agreement. "Tell him that. I keep reminding him we're not getting any younger, but the man wants to believe he's in tip-top health, like he's still in his thirties. Do you know how long it's taken me to get him to schedule his annual physical? Too long."

It's hard picturing either of them slowing down anytime soon. They both have been active in just about anything they do. Dad loves projects outside, and Mom loves volunteering at community functions. They both are constantly on the go doing something for somebody.

She's right, though. They're getting up there and need to pace themselves. Dad is always complaining about his back or his hip hurting but refuses to see a doctor. Mom gets on his case about it until Dad says the same thing he always does when she nags him about scheduling an appointment. *"I'm not spending thirty-five dollars for somebody to tell me I'm old, Maureen.*"

"I'll ask him about swinging by your place to check out whatever you need help with," she relents. "You've never been good with fixing things, so I suppose I'm not surprised the others aren't either."

"I'm handy," I defend.

Mom gives me a pitiful look. "Matty, the Ikea chairs you put together fell apart the first time your father sat in one."

"I put them together right! It's not my fault you bought cheap-ass chairs. They were probably marked down so much because other people had the same problem."

Instead of arguing or pointing out that there *may* have been extra parts after I finished putting them together, she nods in disbelieving reluctance. "Whatever you say, baby. Whatever you say."

I shake my head and let it go.

"How *are* Caleb and his family doing?" she asks. "Your father saw his dad at the store and said he'd been fighting an awful headache that kept making him miss work. I know Caleb has been pulling extra hours at the store to make up for it."

"He's doing all right," I reassure her. Our running back has always gone a hundred miles an hour and still managed to have a healthy relationship and good grades through it all. None of us knows how he does it. "I'll have to get him over here for dinner sometime. I know he and Raine could use a home-cooked meal. Their schedules have been packed."

Mom's face warms. "I'd love to have them. It's been too long since I've seen your friends around. Those boys are like other sons to us."

DJ has been bugging me about Mom's meatloaf, so it's long overdue. "I'll make it happen. I promise."

Checking my watch, I guzzle the rest of the milk, toss the rest of the remaining cookie into my mouth, and walk over to the woman who's shown me nothing but unconditional love all my life. "Thanks for the cookies, Ma."

She startles over my abrupt kiss to the cheek before her surprise melts into a warm smile. "You're leaving already? I was going to make pot roast and mashed potatoes for dinner."

I steal another cookie from the tray. "I'm meeting the guys at Bea's. I'll bring them with me next time. You know DJ can eat an entire roast on his own."

She beams. "Tell them to come this Sunday. I'll put on a ham dinner and make your dad do his brown sugar glaze that's popular. They know they're welcome anytime; they're practically children to me."

It's not the first time I've referred to my friends as siblings. That's how close I am to them. The whole team feels like a family. A dysfunctional one, but still a family.

And family is everything, whether they're blood or chosen.

Which makes me think about Rachel and how far away she is from hers. I couldn't imagine losing my mother, and to be away from the rest of my family would probably kill me. It makes me that much more grateful she's here, willing to be part of the Dragon family when she could choose to be anywhere else.

"I'll tell them," I promise her. "Love you."

I walk out with a new mission that involves a certain brunette I can't stop thinking about, no matter how hard I try.

CHAPTER FOUR

Rachel

STARING AT THE meetings list taped to my office door as I hold my phone between my ear and shoulder and listen to my father drone on, I balk at the new edition written in familiar chicken scratch for a time slot ten minutes from now. It's a clever way to ensure I'll talk to Matthew, considering I've made it a point to distance myself from the charming boy who makes it a point to wiggle his fingers or flash that stupidly annoying white smile at me any chance he gets.

It hasn't been particularly hard to distract myself from the extracurriculars I find myself involved in outside of class and work, thanks to the conversation that seems to be dragging on despite me trying, and failing, to get out of it for the past five minutes.

"...see what the big deal is. It's just a couple of small changes," my father says, sounding as tired as I feel.

A couple of "small" changes doesn't seem to do the situation justice, and my irritation only grows the longer he tries justifying his girlfriend's ideas. "That's the issue, Dad. You don't see the problem. You never do when it comes to Tatum."

God, even saying her name makes my heart hurt. Hell, it

makes me queasy every time I even think about Dad having a girlfriend. It wasn't like I didn't think my father would move on eventually, but my mother hasn't even been gone for nine full months. Not even a *year*! And now he's letting his girlfriend, who's not even ten years older than me, change our Thanksgiving sides the first time she comes to a holiday get-together? It doesn't sit right with me.

Dad sighs heavily for what must be the third time on this call, then mumbles, "I can't keep up with you and your sister. I swear. I can never make everyone happy."

I roll my eyes. He stopped trying to make everybody happy a long time ago. Right around when our mother said goodbye, knowing it was her time to go. A part of him died with her that day, and there was nothing my sister, me, or the therapist we suggested he see could do.

I finagle the lock with my key and use my hip to push open the door and flick on the light. "It's not even about the food," I say. "It's the tradition. We've always done it Mom's way. The holidays were her favorite."

Dad's favorite Thanksgiving side was the yams, Brie's was the macaroni and cheese, and mine was the homemade stuffing. All of them were modified for us—the yams with less sugar for Dad's diabetes, the macaroni and cheese with lactose-free cheese for Brie's intolerance, and the stuffing without raisins because...well, raisins are gross and don't belong in stuffing.

"Traditions can change."

Eye twitching, I drop my belongings onto the desk a little more forcefully than necessary. "It wouldn't be a tradition then, would it?"

I'm greeted with silence.

Rubbing my tired eyes, I unzip my coat and peel it off one arm at a time. "This is our first Thanksgiving without her, and you're letting your girlfriend change the menu we've served for years. Did you even think to stop and consider how that makes us feel—how it would make *Mom* feel?"

I hear the subtle intake of breath from the other side of the phone, like I sucker punched him in the gut. But after my sister called me to vent about Tatum coming over for Thanksgiving and how she suggested getting rid of the yams and macaroni and cheese to make things "simpler" to prepare, I couldn't just let it go.

Tradition is tradition for a reason.

"Do you honestly think I've forgotten that my wife is dead?" he snaps in a voice I've never heard him use before.

I blink at the coolness I can feel from hundreds of miles away. And I certainly don't ease the growing tension by replying, "I don't know, Dad. You tell me. You're the one who moved on from her. Not us."

The second I say it, I close my eyes, knowing I crossed a line. And I cringe when the call ends abruptly.

"Shit," I mumble, pulling the phone away from my ear to see the blank screen.

He hung up on me.

"That sounded intense," a familiar voice says quietly from the doorway.

I turn to see Matt standing there.

The meeting.

I already forgot.

Pinching the bridge of my nose, I push my glasses up

and set my phone on my desk. "Family problems," I tell him distantly, eventually pulling my chair back from the desk and taking a seat.

He stays at the doorway. "Tell me about them."

His words take me by surprise. "Trust me, I don't want to bore you with my personal issues. That isn't why you're here."

Slowly, he nods. "You're right. It isn't." Lifting a shoulder, he walks in and sits across from me, dropping his bag on the ground beside him. "But it looks like you could use somebody to talk to, and I'm here."

He really wants to listen to me rant? I'm sure he'd rather do anything else. "Matt…"

"No ulterior motive," he promises. "Just you and me talking about whatever has those eyes dulled. Talk to me, Rach."

I stare at him for a long time, unblinking, not breathing, heart slowly increasing in my chest with an ache that settled there after my father hung up on me.

Then I feel my jaw quiver. "She wants to get rid of the yams!" I bellow, feeling tears spring into my eyes before I can fight them off.

Matt's eyes widen at the outburst. "What?"

"The yams," I repeat as if he knows what I'm talking about, his image becoming blurry from the tears building in the ducts. "My father's girlfriend wants to get rid of the yams, the mac and cheese, and probably the stuffing too! We always did those sides, and she wants to change everything."

Slowly, so slowly, Matt nods as he soaks in the rushed answer. He reaches forward to grab a tissue from the box I keep on the desk and passes it to me. It's only then I realize a few tears have slid down my cheek.

I blot the tissue against my face and take a deep breath. "It's the first Thanksgiving without our mother," I tell him quietly, staring at the damp Kleenex in my hand.

Sympathy clouds Matt's otherwise soft features. "I didn't realize she died recently."

All I can do is nod, feeling the lump in my throat grow bigger and bigger.

His voice is uncharacteristically soft. "You said she was sick. Can I ask what it is she had?"

I peek at him through my damp lashes and try blinking away the tears. Sniffling, I clear my throat and tear apart the tissue in my hands. "It's called Huntington's disease. It's a rare neurodegenerative disorder that basically causes your brain cells to decay over time. There isn't one part of a person's life that isn't impacted by it. They just slowly deteriorate in front of everyone they love."

His lips curl deeper at the corners. "And there's no cure?"

Silently, I shake my head.

Mom's disease was a slow progression that occurred silently for years before it became a physical problem. She played it off as if it was nothing but a slight inconvenience anytime she forgot basic things, started tripping and falling, or got moody over stuff she never used to react to. By the time any of us realized it was serious, it was too late.

Dad used to beat himself up over not seeing the signs sooner, not that any of us knew what Huntington's was before her. She wasn't close to her side of the family, so she never knew the health history.

"Damn, Rach. That's…that's tough."

All I can do is nod. Words can't describe watching the person who was the most hands-on with us worsen every day, knowing there's nothing you can do about it.

Matt wets his lips when he sees me burying myself in the pain of my reality. Then he says, "I was adopted."

I gape at him. "What?"

He nods once. "I was adopted when I was a baby. Not many people know that. It's not a secret, but it's not something I advertise either."

I've seen his parents at games. He looks a lot like his father, so I never would have guessed.

He lifts his shoulders nonchalantly. "I don't know anything about my birth family because it was a closed adoption. All I have are my assumptions as to why they gave me up. They were young, probably. Maybe not in the best head-space to raise a kid. So they gave me a chance to have a good life. I'll always be grateful for that."

I stop tearing apart the tissue. "Have you ever thought about finding out?"

"Once in a while, I think about it," he admits softly, looking at the wall with a contemplative expression on his face. "But then I think about the people who brought me up and taught me what love is. There's a chance I wouldn't have had those circumstances if I were raised by anybody else."

I watch him as he stares off, thinking about who knows what. "That's sweet," I tell him, clearing my raspy throat. "I know how much they love you. I can see it every time they come to watch you play."

He meets my eyes with a gentle smile.

"I loved my mother more than anything," I tell him, my voice thick with emotion as I picture her in my head. Her bright smile and brighter eyes tease my consciousness and make me miss her ten times more.

Brie and I look identical to our mother, which our father always said was a blessing and a curse because Mom had the type of beauty that could have won her any pageant she entered. Thankfully, she passed her brownie-batter brown hair, hazel-green eyes, and peach skin to us instead of Dad's thin black hair, brown eyes, and paleness. Everything from our short five-foot height to the lean build of our bodies to the way we tan in the summertime is a reminder of what Lorelei Holloway left behind.

"And I know she loved us too," I add, staring down at my lap. "But my father…He went from grieving her to moving on like it meant nothing. And now he's got a girlfriend that he wants us to meet, and it makes me wonder if he ever really loved her at all."

I never used to question it. My parents were the sickening, sweet couple that gave people cavities just looking at them. But how could someone move on so quickly the way my father did if it were actually love? They were together for almost three decades. That seems like a lot of history to just…forget.

"Maybe your dad is coping with the loss by trying to distract himself from the hurt. We all grieve differently."

Rubbing my lips together, I think about it. "I think my mother was the super glue our family needed to stick together. Because now…" I lift my shoulders dejectedly.

The way Matt watches me should make me squirm, but

there's something light in his blue-gray eyes that calms me instead. "You're mad at your dad."

That's the easiest way to put it. "I feel a lot of things toward my father, and anger is definitely one of them. But I'm more confused than anything. Hurt. It makes me wonder what love really is if he could find somebody else so quickly after the woman he said was the love of his life."

He nods in understanding, his eyes going to my phone when it lights up. "Avoiding him won't answer those questions, you know."

He's not wrong, but that doesn't make me want to talk to the man I have conflicted feelings over.

"Look," he says, scooting forward in his seat and resting his elbows on his knees. "There's a lot I wish I knew about my birth family. I've long since accepted that I probably never will. That's not to say I don't feel lucky and grateful for the family I got. I'll never properly be able to put into words how much I am. But your father is still here, still alive. You'll regret shutting him out or being mad at him forever. Family is too important to live without them, Rach."

My phone starts going off again.

"You should answer that," he encourages, his chin gesturing toward the cell phone I've been ignoring.

"It's your time," I answer, my eyes dipping to the screen briefly before returning to him.

A small smile graces his lips when my eyes go back down to the flashing phone with my father's name on it.

He grabs his bag and takes something wrapped in white tissue paper from it. "I came to give you this."

I hesitantly accept the light offering with furrowed brows

as I see the red fabric peeking through.

Matt moves the paper aside to reveal my last name stitched onto the back of a jersey that looks identical to the ones they wear. "I had it custom-made for you. You're an honorary Dragon. Part of the family. Don't let the number offend you; I had to figure out one that wouldn't be used during the game."

My eyes roam over the double zero beneath my name. Emotion builds in the back of my throat that I have to clear away. "You did this for me?"

"Nobody else here with your last name," the wide receiver points out with a grin. "It's the least I could do. You've done a lot for us this semester."

He's quiet for a second as I stare at the present I wasn't expecting.

Clearing his throat, he rubs the back of his neck and adds, "I talked to my mom the other day and realized that this team is like a second family. And it seemed like maybe you could use that. Now more than ever, I guess."

My eyes dart to where he stands, his weight shifting from one foot to another as I study his soft features. "Thank you," I whisper.

"You should start coming to the games again. We seem to suck without you there," he muses, pointing to the jersey. "Make sure to wear that. It could be our lucky charm."

Emotion crams into my throat.

He walks to the door. "You should call your dad back too."

I watch as he leaves, giving me no other excuse to ignore my father.

I stare at the thoughtful gift, running my fingers along the stitched name.

Then I pick up the phone.

Dad says, "I'm sorry."

There's a long pause from me.

Then I say, "I'm sorry too."

And a little weight lifts from my chest.

The day before Thanksgiving break, a can of yams is sitting on my desk with no note. Not that I need one after my outburst.

That night, I go to the game in my brand-new jersey and support the team—my Lindon family.

They win.

Then I drive to Pennsylvania for the holidays, meet Dad's girlfriend, and my little sister and I make the side dishes our mother would be proud of as our father watched with glassy eyes.

It's not much.

But it's a start.

CHAPTER FIVE

Rachel

L INDON'S POPULATION WAS made up of a whopping 4,082 people during the last census, with an additional 5,380 students who attended the local university during the college season. None of that is relevant information until I realize how small that truly makes the town when it's full of twenty-somethings looking for a good time.

"I'm sorry," I apologize to my date for the third time when I see the boys in the corner making kissy faces in my direction. "I work with the university football team, and the players can be a little...rambunctious."

My date is a twenty-seven-year-old car salesman who I matched with on a dating app like a total loser because I never get out long enough to meet people organically. The men in my graduate classes aren't anything to write home about and the guys I deal with when I'm working are a handful of years younger than my twenty-four.

Even if the Thanksgiving and Christmas holidays with Dad and Tatum weren't totally awful, I didn't want to follow in my father's footsteps and rob the cradle.

But after the new year came and went, and the Upstate New York winter stretched on and made everything cold, dark, and miserable, I found myself wanting...something.

And since the temptation to go after the one person who would be more than happy to warm my bed was constantly around me on campus, I decided to do something about it.

So, after a very lackluster Valentine's Day alone, I decided to sign up for a few dating apps that my sister insisted I try.

Dylan, who's been talking about how he won employee of the month three times in a row, frowns at the boys making a scene. "Are you sure you wouldn't rather be over there? Seems like they want you to be."

If Matthew Clearwater had anything to say about it, I'd be occupying the empty seat beside him. "I'm fine right here. So, tell me more about your five-year plan."

He gives one last feigning glance at the obnoxious athletes before turning to me and grabbing his beer. "I'm going to move to California to work for Google. Hopefully, my future wife will raise our kids as a stay-at-home mom. You know, the dream."

I blink at the nineteen-fifties throwback, trying my hardest not to flinch.

There's nothing wrong with being a stay-at-home mother. It's a full-time job in itself, but it's definitely not *my* dream. Not that he asks, but I indulge him with my own plans. "I'm in grad school to get my master's in sports psychology. Maybe I'll work with other sports teams in the future, but I think it would be fun to become a professor and teach as an adjunct or maybe become some sort of counselor. Hopefully, in five years, I'll have my doctorate with enough teaching experience to get something full-time. Tenure would be nice if I decide on the education track."

My date sips his beer, his eyes glancing in the direction of the flatscreen playing a football game before coming back to me. "What kind of focus is sports psychology? Seems like a throwaway major people choose when they don't want to become regular therapists."

His answer causes heat to prickle the back of my head and ears. "Athletes get put through the wringer to get where they are. It can be mentally taxing on them, especially if their goal is to go pro. I'd like to help them. If I can."

"How do you feel about California?"

"Uh…" I stop myself, a little irritated he has nothing to say to my original response. "It seems dry. And hot. I've never really thought about the West Coast that much if I'm being honest. It's a little out of my price range."

He hums, looking from the television playing to the table of boys who are still wiggling their fingers suggestively at us. "What exactly do you do with them?"

His weirdly worded question makes my eyes twitch. "What do you mean? I advise them. Make sure they're on top of their schoolwork so they can keep playing. That sort of thing."

Another unreadable noise comes from him as he finishes off his beer. "It's strange, is all. You're young and attractive. Doesn't seem like you'd fit into that world, especially not with a bunch of horned-up jocks. I'd know. I was one back in the day."

Back in the day. As if this guy is decades older than me rather than four years.

My lips twitch. "It's not like they're walking around sporting boners all the time. They come into my office, I tell them what they need to do to keep their GPA up, and then they leave. Half of them don't even listen to me."

He doesn't need to know the times Matthew will come in and flirt with me, because it's playful at best. Innocent. Ish. Until it wasn't.

The man across from me shakes his head, sliding the empty Corona bottle away. "If you were my girlfriend, I wouldn't want you being around them at all. Even for a paycheck. Guys are too untrustworthy, especially at that age."

"Wouldn't you trust your girlfriend?"

"It's not about that," he argues.

I don't see how it isn't. The more he talks, the more he reminds me of my high school boyfriend, Michael. He'd wanted to settle down and live the all-American dream that would have left *my* dreams on the back burner. As much as I thought I loved him, I loved building a future for myself more. Which meant exploring something outside of the relationship I'd been comfortable in.

"Sounds like it's a good thing I'm not your girlfriend then," I reply tartly, grateful I didn't accept the second drink he offered to buy me.

The man, who I initially thought was cute before he opened his mouth, stands. "I think the date is over."

The only thing I do is nod, watching him grab his jacket and phone and head toward the door without another word or look my way. When he disappears behind it, I slump back into my seat and feel a little embarrassed that my bad date is witnessed by people I see multiple times a week.

Another failed date to tell my sister about.

Fun.

A few moments later, a pink drink with sugar on the rim and a lime wedged on the edge is set in front of me. "I didn't order—"

"He was a douche," Matt says, sliding the same drink I ordered before closer to me on the napkin. "You deserve better."

Instead of taking the drink, I lean back and look to the twenty-one-year-old who celebrated his birthday over the winter break. "And how would you know what I deserve, Matthew?"

He simply lifts a shoulder. "I know that you looked miserable every time that guy opened his mouth. He cut you off twice. Never responded to anything you said about yourself. And he rolled his eyes when you ordered the passionfruit margarita. I don't have to know a lot about you to know that nobody deserves to be treated that way, *Ms. Holloway.*"

Eyes drifting to the drink he got for me, I stifle a sigh and push it away. "Thank you, but I can't accept this. It would be inappropriate."

He gestures toward his teammates. "As far as I'm concerned, this is coincidental. We all happen to be at Fishtail at the same time. It doesn't have to be a big thing, so you should come join us and have your drink."

Why wouldn't it be coincidental? Eyes narrowing at the tall blond, I ask, "Did you know I was going to be here?"

I've been around long enough to know where the local hangouts are for students. Fishtail is usually only popular on Tuesdays and Fridays when everything is half off. It's a

Thursday night at seven thirty—hardly partying time.

Matt's lips kick up at the corners. "Try not to be too offended, Ruby Red. When we like someone, we want to make sure they're being treated with respect. I may have suggested we come here when I overheard you on the phone telling your sister about your date yesterday when the guys and I were heading to the locker room. But it's good that I came since he was a jackass."

"Be nice," I chide, even though my date definitely does not deserve any defending. He *was* a jackass.

Matt shakes his head. "You're too nice for your own good. Why are you giving losers like him a shot anyway?"

"Why does anybody date?" I ask, crossing my arms.

He watches me for a second. "There are a lot of reasons. Boredom. Loneliness. Sex."

I swallow at the last one, my thighs tightening at the thought of him between them.

Matt leans toward me. "Which one is the reason you're here?"

He's definitely not getting an answer. "Why are *you* here? You must have better things to do than spy on your adviser."

One of his shoulders lifts casually. "Not really. I've got the whole night to kill."

Of course he does. "So you cleared your schedule to watch me fail at dating? Great." I mumble the last part.

Matt taps the table to get my attention. "There isn't anything wrong with dating for those reasons, you know. I'm not judging. I've definitely dated for all of them at one point or another. And, for the record, it isn't like I wanted your date to go bad. He was an ass and doesn't deserve you."

I don't want to think about that. "I wanted to put myself out there, is all. Be normal. Find something to do outside of work and school."

"Understandable."

I look at the margarita he bought me. "My sister is getting married over our spring break. She keeps hounding me about if I'm bringing a date."

If I find one, great. If I don't...Well, there's a reason I didn't want to get my hopes up. I was doing this for me, not for the sake of checking "plus one" off on the RSVP, no matter how excited Brie would be if I told her I was bringing somebody.

"Any good prospects?" he presses.

I look at him and his boyish smirk that makes mischief flash in his gray-blue eyes. "Not so far," I tell him.

He hums, watching me carefully. Then he picks up the margarita, gesturing toward the table he secured in the corner. "Come on. You can hang out and have some actual fun with people you like for a change."

Realistically, I should have known he was eavesdropping on my conversation with my sister about tonight. By the time I saw him outside my door, Daniel and Caleb were tugging him along, saying something about not creeping on me. I brushed it off because I was excited about my night out. Dylan seemed like a decent person when we talked online.

Matt stops when he sees I'm not following him. "Come on, Rach. We don't bite. You and I both know you can handle your own with the guys. And chances are, they're going to be on their best behavior with you around versus if you leave. That means less chances of you having to hear Pearce yelling at us tomorrow if we show up hungover."

Rubbing my lips together, I weigh my options. I know the smart thing to do would be to grab my jacket, purse, and phone, and go home.

Instead, I find myself grabbing my things and following the wide receiver to the table of his peers, who hoot and holler when I stop by the empty seat next to Matthew's.

It's probably a good thing Aiden decided to drop out to train for the combine, or he'd be here reminding everybody that this isn't a good idea.

"Welcome to the mayhem, Rach," one of the boys greets.

What are you doing? the logical voice inside my head asks.

I squash it with a sip of my drink.

Having fun, I answer.

I don't think about Dylan the rest of the night.

CHAPTER SIX

Matt

T HE FIRST DAY back from spring break is the reason for the dull ache in my head that throbs as I gear up for another day of practice. Coach Pearce is out for vengeance after our growing losing streak, and it's made our time on the field brutal. Spring break was a desperately needed week away from the man who was working our asses off to the point of pure exhaustion.

"You shouldn't have convinced me to do that last shot of Jager," I tell DJ, feeling queasy as I slide my helmet on and pray I don't vomit in it. I happen to know what that smells like even after approximately ten washes.

It doesn't smell good.

"Convinced you?" DJ snorts, grabbing his water bottle and taking a sip before opening the locker room door. "You reached for that shot all on your own, buddy. Then you tried telling *me* to do another one with you. I saved both of our livers by saying no."

God, I feel like shit right now.

I'm pretty sure DJ and I crushed a twelve-pack of Pabst Blue Ribbon, finished what was left in the bottle of Jack Daniels we swiped from the kitchen, and did at least three shots of Jager during the party we had to celebrate our last break of the semester.

Based on how moody he's been lately, I'm pretty sure he needed to let loose as much as I did. Especially since his shoulder injury took him out for the season. I feel for him. He wanted to end his senior year on top, and now he can't. I'd be pissy too.

His shoulder isn't his only issue though. He's got beef with Wallace that's left them at each other's throats for weeks. DJ has been taking it out on our quarterback and copping attitude to Coach Pearce every chance he gets. I've never seen him like it before.

I haven't pressed him for the details on whatever is souring his mood, but I know the reason isn't good. Caleb knows more than I do because he's the go-to guy for people to confide in. Whatever it is seems to be serious enough to kill DJ's usually chipper personality, and I have a feeling it has to do with Skylar—the cute blonde he got involved with at the beginning of the semester.

But if I ask him what's wrong, it would open doors for him to pry into my business. I don't want that. Because then I'd have to tell him that I'm being a moody bastard about a woman I have no right being so hung up on.

"I don't want another drop of alcohol anytime soon," I groan, trying to push off the thought. I hold my stomach as it gurgles its threats.

DJ snickers at my pain. "You say that every year and then invite us all out to Fishtail like a week later. Drink some water and try not to puke on the field. You'll be fine."

He smacks my back, making me bite down on my tongue before the greasy lunch I forced down comes back up.

Shooting him a glare, he chuckles and nods toward the light on in the office we're approaching. "Look who's back," he says, stopping by the door. "Hi, Rach. Long time no talk. Miss us?"

Rachel looks up from where she's sitting behind her desk. She looks...different. Her glasses are gone, her hair is a little lighter and shorter, and she's wearing minimal makeup, if any at all. She looks far more comfortable now than she did when I first met her last semester, with her ass bent over the desk in that tight outfit of hers that played a starring role in many cold showers.

"Hi, Daniel," she greets before her eyes move over to me. Her smile doesn't falter, but I can't help but sense she loses a light in her eyes. "Hi, Matthew."

Matthew. Not Matt. "Have a good break?" I ask, as if I didn't stalk her a little online to see what she was up to in the whopping nine days we were away.

I know she looked beautiful in the dress she wore to her sister's wedding. She was tagged by a few people in the bridal party the days leading up to the spring ceremony, including a man named Michael, who looked a little too chummy for my liking based on the picture he shared of them sitting together with his arm stretched out across the chair behind her. His profile is locked down tighter than Fort Knox when I tried looking into him, so I have no idea who he is.

And it's probably for the better.

Rachel toys with the pen in her hand. "I did. How about you two?"

"Minus the killer hangover we're sporting thanks to this

one," DJ nudges me in the ribs with his elbow, "it wasn't bad. Could have been worse."

He pulls his phone out of his back pocket when it buzzes, making him frown. "I gotta go. See you later, Rach."

When it's the two of us, we remain in a thick silence that has me sighing.

Then we both start talking at the same time. I ask, "How was the wedding?" at the same time she asks me, "Is Daniel okay?"

Scratching my neck, I glance to where DJ disappeared around the corner. I guess anyone who's been around him knows he hasn't been himself. "I'm not sure, to be honest. Something is going on with him."

She nods, her eyes going to the doorway beyond me, deep in thought. "Maybe it has to do with his injury. I'll see if he wants to have a meeting. I know he's out for the rest of the season so he can have surgery, so it might be bothering him."

He loves the game. When we were freshmen, he talked about going pro like Griffith did, except only one of them ever had a real shot. Mostly thanks to DJ's fucked-up shoulder. But also because Coach Pearce spent more time conditioning Griff for the game than he ever spent on anybody else.

"I'm not entirely sure, but I think there's something happening between him and Wallace," I tell her, taking off my helmet. "It goes beyond everybody being pissed at his arrogance, but I don't know the full story."

Rachel frowns. "I'll look into it, especially if it's affecting him and the team."

I nod because that's all I can do. Looking around the office as if I've never been in here before, I take my time to fill the silence I'm greeted with again. Then I say, "You might want to talk to Caleb too. He probably knows more than I do."

Rachel's soft smile curls her lips. "I will."

We're quiet again.

"So, how was the wedding?"

I don't know why I want to torture myself by hearing about who she went with, but curiosity has nipped at my stomach since I saw the photo of her with the mystery guy. They were both smiling, and it hardly seemed fake. I know what her feigned smiles look like by now.

She drops the pen on her desk. "It was good. Brie is a happily married woman now, and I'm happy for her."

Not sure if I should bring it up, I shift my weight and glance at the picture frame of her, her sister, and her mother that's resting on the corner of her desk. "Did you ever find a date?"

Rachel only meets my eyes for a brief second before turning her chair to her computer. "No, I didn't."

I stare, fighting the flare in my nostrils when irritation takes over. She lied. Why would she lie?

Clearing her throat, she says, "I do have some work to catch up on, though. I'll send out emails to everyone with their next meeting date to go over grad school applications and end-of-the-year reports. Let the boys know."

She's dismissing me.

Gripping my helmet, I turn toward the door.

"I'll ask around about things with DJ and Wallace," she

promises, as if that's the only thing I want from her.

Jaw ticking, I head to the field and get my ass kicked again, thanks to Pearce's shitty mood that only makes mine worse.

BEA'S BAKERY IS bustling the next morning, with a line twice as long as normal since Ivy quit to go away with Griffith. It left Bea and her teenage granddaughter, Elena, in charge of everything and looking for help that never seemed to last more than a month or two at most.

The bubbly teen waves at me from behind the counter, not looking nearly as stressed as the last girl they hired to replace Ivy. I'm fairly certain the constant demands of various coffees and pastries made the poor girl cry on her second day. Bea had told her to go home, sending her with lavender tea to relax. I never saw the girl again after that.

For a while, the running joke the guys and I went with was that Bea poisoned her. When the older woman heard that, she smacked us upside the heads and told us to hush. She never denied it though.

When it's finally my turn, I say, "You need to hire someone."

Elena makes a sour face. "Tell my grandma that," she grumbles. "She won't listen to me. I'm pretty sure she's broken, like, five child labor laws by now with the hours I'm working here. How am I supposed to have a life?"

I'm happy Bea's place is always busy because that means she's doing well, but I get it. If I were in Elena's shoes, I'd probably be upset too if I was always here. "I can try talking to her if you want," I offer.

She beams. "Really?"

"Don't get your hopes up," I warn knowingly. "We both know your grandma is a stubborn woman. If she's set on something, she sticks to it. She might not listen."

Bea walks out of the back, wiping her hands off on a dish towel. "Listen to what?"

Elena rubs her lips together.

I sigh. "I told her you guys need to hire somebody for extra help. You've been packed lately."

"You don't see me complaining," Bea comments, eyeing the teenager rocking on her heels behind the register. "Weren't you hoping to buy a car? I'm giving you the hours you want. It's not going to be cheap."

Elena frowns. "I know it won't be, but…"

Bea's brows arch in wait.

Her granddaughter groans. "I just get sick of this place sometimes. My friends are always asking if I want to go out with them but I'm usually busy here. What if I want to date? I could be missing out on my soulmate right now, Grandma. Do you want me to die a bitter old woman with fifty cats?"

Bea rolls her eyes. "You're barely seventeen. You have a while before you need to start worrying about that. In fact, the only thing you should be concerning yourself with is asking him what he wants to drink."

Elena blows out a long breath as Bea walks around the counter and checks on the different tables of people eating.

I cringe, giving her a told-you-so face before offering a sympathetic smile. "If it makes you feel any better, relationships early on in life hardly ever work anyway. You're better off soulmate searching when you're older and focusing on school and getting a car for now."

She frowns. "You sound like my parents."

I pull out a twenty after telling her what coffee I'd like. "I was your age once, not that long ago. I know where you're at, but trust me on this." When she passes me back the change, I tuck it all in the tip jar. "For your future investment," I tell her with a smile.

Elena gawks at the seventeen dollars and change I put in there. As she prepares my drink, she asks, "Have you found her yet?"

My brows pinch. "Who?"

"Your soulmate," she elaborates. "The infamous one. Whatever you want to call it. You said to wait until I'm older. Are you looking?"

I'd hardly say that's on my to-do list, but that doesn't mean I haven't thought about what life after college looks like. And who it looks like with. "I'm not so sure I've been actively searching," I tell the teen.

Interest piques on her face. "That doesn't mean you haven't found her."

I accept the coffee cup she slides my way, watching the steam billow from the plastic opening on the top. "That doesn't mean I have either," I answer, picking up the drink and lifting it in goodbye. "Good luck with your grandma."

"Good luck with soulmate searching," she calls out loudly, gaining a few onlookers' attention as I walk out the door.

Shaking my head, I push the door open and think more about what comes after I graduate in a short few months.

The problem is…I don't know.

CHAPTER SEVEN

Rachel

I T TAKES LESS than five minutes to see that Daniel Bridges Junior is going through it. "How is your shoulder?" I ask him as he rolls it. Something pops, making him wince.

The team's wide receiver, or I suppose former wide receiver since his injury took him out indefinitely, sinks into the chair. "Hurts like a bitch sometimes."

"Do they need to do a second surgery?"

He had one in December, and I know he's had to do some physical therapy and exercises on his own time to help the recovery process. "No, they don't think that's necessary. I go back for a checkup in a couple weeks to make sure."

I'm not used to him being so solemn. "I'm going to cut to the chase because you're not being yourself. Where is the hyper boy who was always bouncing off the walls when we first met?"

He stares down at his lap, lifting his good shoulder in a half-shrug. "There's been a lot going on, Rach. That's all."

There's more to it than that. "Is it because of your shoulder? I know you were upset you couldn't finish the season with the team."

Daniel scowls, his face scrunching up as he keeps his eyes facing his lap. "It's not even a team anymore. Not like it was."

My brows arch inquisitively. "Why do you say that? Because Aiden and Justin aren't on it anymore?"

He hesitates, his fist scrunching and uncrunching over the arm of the chair. "Because Pearce isn't doing shit to make it one," he replies coolly.

Slowly, I nod. I've heard some murmurings that Daniel has been picking fights with the head coach. Nobody seems to know the reason why. Or if they do, they aren't sharing. "Okay…What do you mean, exactly?"

He sighs, finally meeting my eyes. "It doesn't take a genius to see that Wallace is Pearce's new favorite. He's always had them. With Griff gone, he needed somebody new to focus on. But Wallace is a prick who thinks he can get away with anything, and—" His face gets all red, and the tendons in his neck pulse.

"Take a deep breath," I tell him gently.

Daniel takes a few seconds before inhaling and closing his eyes to exhale.

"Look, I know Ricky isn't a fan favorite among the guys," I begin, getting a dry snort from him in return. "But he's still on the team. Is there something that happened that you want to talk about? Because you've never been the type to get yourself involved in petty drama just because of somebody's ego before."

He's quiet, his jaw grinding from the question. Which tells me I'm right. There is something. And I don't know why he isn't telling me when I've always tried to be on their side.

"DJ," I say carefully, earning me another glance. I rarely,

if ever, call him that. It's the nickname for him only the boys use. "You can talk to me. I'm here to help, remember?"

His fingers tap against the armchair for a minute before he abruptly stands. "Wallace isn't a good guy. That's what's wrong. And Pearce isn't doing shit about it."

"Maybe I can talk—"

"No. I'll figure it out on my own." He walks out the door without another look in my direction, leaving me gaping at the empty chair that he occupied.

I blink.

Then blink again.

"Okay," I say slowly, shaking my head.

A few hours later, when Caleb comes to a one-on-one about grad school applications, I ask him about Daniel. The frown I'm greeted with tells me it's even worse than I anticipated.

And when he tells me the rumors he's been hearing about Wallace possibly drugging girls at parties, my stomach dips. Could Couch Pearce really know about that and not do anything just because Ricky is his newest protégé?

I make him the same promise I do to Matt. That I'll look into it. Because I can tell Caleb is worried about Daniel as much as I am.

After that, we discuss his future plans.

Grad school and Anders Hardware. I help him with applications, and he goes on his way.

Matt doesn't show up for his meeting, so I pack up and go home after twenty-five minutes of waiting around.

⭐

TWO DAYS LATER, I knock on Coach Pearce's office door to see him going over something on his computer.

The fifty-two-year-old man is married despite his cool demeanor, which makes his personality a little lacking. This makes me wonder what his home life is like since he's so stoic here.

I've had plenty of bosses who intimidated me in the past, like the middle-aged woman going through a mid-life crisis who ran the frozen yogurt shop when I was sixteen or the creepy old guy who constantly made passes at the waitstaff who managed the diner I worked at when I was eighteen. I'm used to dealing with easily agitated people, so this time is no different.

"Coach Pearce?" I say, feeling a little uncomfortable. I have a plan. Not a great one, but a plan, nonetheless.

The man behind the desk doesn't look up when he grunts out, "What is it?"

Hesitating, I step into his office. "I was hoping to talk to you about a couple of things. I know that two of the players have birthdays during summer break, so I was thinking we could do something for them before the semester officially ends since they've celebrated each other's birthdays through-out the season. That way, nobody feels left out. We could order some pizza and maybe do a cake."

Coach Pearce pauses what he's doing, looking over at me. "Rachel, right?"

I nod slowly. We've worked together long enough to know one another's name. "Yes, sir."

"Well, Rachel, this isn't Chuck E. Cheese; this is a college. I'm sure the boys will have their own parties on their off time. They'll have an entire summer to celebrate."

I'd expected as much, so I wet my lips and try to convince him otherwise. "I get that, but I read this article once about how important it is to boost morale by—"

"Does it look like I care?"

No. No, it doesn't. Still, I try. "If you don't want to do something for their birthdays, we could do something for the team. Like a team dinner. It can be a bonding experience. I've heard about the tension between some of the players. It seems like there's a lot of intensity between Ricky Wallace and—"

"It's not your job to concern yourself with *my* players," he cuts me off pointedly.

I swallow down my words. For a second.

"Isn't it my job to ensure they're on their best behavior? Doing their work? Getting good grades? Being present on the field? If there are things going on off the field, it translates to their playing time. We've both seen the impact outside drama brings into the games."

Coach Pearce stares at me like I told him we should hire strippers before the game. Which I'm sure they would like a lot more than a pizza party, but that's beside the point. "When I said I needed a new athletic adviser, it wasn't so they could plan parties for my players. The boys can do that all on their own. All I need from you is to make sure they pass their classes so I don't have to kick them off the team. Not butt into business that isn't yours or host shit that's unnecessary. Is that understood?"

Pressing my lips together, I nod once at his scathing reprimanding.

"And a little advice," he says, turning back to his computer. "Don't treat them like your friends. You're a faculty member. You shouldn't be anything else to them. What they do outside of your office isn't anything you need to insert yourself into. Am I clear?"

My face grows warm at the warning. He doesn't want me prying, and God only knows what he'd do if he found out I was. But a nagging feeling has me debating on risking it anyway.

Daniel wouldn't be so torn up if this didn't impact him or someone he cares about somehow, and the claims against Ricky are too serious to just ignore because the head coach isn't interested in involving himself in investigating them.

"I do understand," I say, still standing at the doorway despite the obvious dismissal he's giving me. "But I want what's best for the Dragons too. That's why I'm bringing it up."

Pearce slowly looks back over at me, dumbfounded that I'm still talking. "I don't know how much clearer I can get with you. It's not your job to do what's best for the team. That's mine."

My nostrils flare open as I glance at the floor.

I stand there for a few moments longer before turning on my heel when I realize he's got nothing left to say. No more warnings or cold scoldings. He's said his piece.

If I were smart, I'd listen to him.

But my gut tugs me in a different direction.

A few days later, four large pizzas are delivered to the screening room, where the guys watch game tapes. Two separate cards wait for the players whose birthdays are coming up next to a small marble cake I bought at the store before coming in for class.

I don't join them for a lot of reasons. One, because Pearce is probably angry. And two, it leaves them all distracted for me to dig even though I told myself I shouldn't.

But Ricky Wallace even gives *me* a weird feeling in my stomach, and my intuition has rarely been wrong. So, I go against the rules for a second time because of a player. Except this time, it's for illegally accessing personal files to try to get some answers to questions flying around the locker room that Pearce refuses to acknowledge.

If that's how I go down, I'll be okay with it.

Because at least I was trying to do something right for once.

The Lindon Dragons are a family.

My family.

And like Matt said before.

Family is important.

CHAPTER EIGHT
Matt

M Y BODY ACHES like it always does the day after practice, making me wince with every step I take down Main Street. At least Bea gave me an extra-large coffee on the house when she saw how rough I looked when I dragged my ass into her bakery with DJ.

The dickhead in question snickers when he elbows me in the ribs after seeing my hunched over reflection in the glass window of Anders Hardware—Caleb's family business.

Listening to the front door chime as we swing it open, we approach the counter with two extra coffees for Caleb and his father. I note the way Mr. Anders pushes his glasses up his nose and tries following along to whatever Caleb is explaining to him on the computer.

"Looking a little pale today, Mr. A," DJ notes, grabbing a sucker from the display case and tossing a dollar bill for it onto the counter. "I think you and the missus need a vacation somewhere sunny."

Caleb's dad has been looking a little tired lately, but they've been working a lot more to get Caleb ready to take over the store now that graduation is looming. Last I heard, he wants his son to be in charge seventy percent of the time by this time next year. I doubt the old man from whom my best friend gets his looks from will retire anytime soon, but he's mentioned that being the ultimate goal in the next ten years.

I set the coffees down in front of them.

"No time for sunshine," Mr. Anders claims, rubbing his head. "Too much to do. And the price of lumber is jacked up these days, making it harder to get new stock delivered here for people. It's giving me a damn headache."

Caleb rolls his eyes as he takes the caffeine offering. "Everything gives you a headache these days. The other day, we tried ordering incandescent lightbulbs, and he started going off about how much he hates the government because he couldn't find any."

I chuckle. "The government, huh?"

Mr. A turns to us. "Goddamn inflation makes everything too high. Nothing is worth it these days. Everybody says to support the local economy, but it's the little guys getting screwed over. Tell me I'm wrong."

DJ and I both hold our palms up in surrender. He won't be getting an argument from either of us.

Caleb pats his dad's arm and passes him the other coffee cup. "Why don't you head out? Mom said she was making your favorite tonight for dinner. I'll close up before the guys and I go out."

His father frowns, contemplating a reason to stay, before eventually relenting and taking the drink we got him. "All right. I should take some aspirin anyway and get some sleep. You boys, don't stay up too late; you've got a big game coming up."

DJ salutes him, even though he doesn't have to worry

about his skills on the field. "We'd never think of it, sir."

That's bullshit, and everybody in this room knows it. Out of all of us, DJ is the one constantly encouraging us to stay out longer by buying everybody more rounds of drinks after we tell him it's time to go. We're broke, so none of us ever want to turn down a drink that's been paid for.

It's basic boy math.

After his father leaves, Caleb turns to us with a frown. "I think there's something wrong with my dad. He's not himself."

DJ hops onto the counter, shoving his sucker into his mouth. "The dude is stressed. His son is graduating, and he's got a business to run. I don't know how he does it."

Caleb shakes his head, and I can tell whatever he's noticed is concerning him. "I don't know, man. It seems like it's more than that. Mom and I have been telling him to see a doctor, but you know how he is. He's too stubborn. Every time we bring it up, he makes an excuse not to go. The store. My football games. The holidays. Birthdays. You name it. I'm worried."

I've never seen Caleb like this before. "Your mom should make him an appointment and bring him. That's what my parents do. I'm sure he won't go on his own, but we all know he'd do anything for her. If she brought him there, he'd hardly put up a fight."

When DJ sees the seriousness shadowing Caleb's face, he quickly nods. "Matt has a point. If you need store coverage, you know we can help out whenever he gets seen."

Caleb's shoulders drop. "Thanks, guys. I'll let you know. Anyway, let me finish up a few things, and then we can head out. Are we going to Fishtail? I heard they're having a ribeye special tonight."

I happen to know that our adviser has another date at Fiesta because I may or may not have been eavesdropping on her the other day. I hadn't meant to. I was going to her office to apologize for missing my meeting, but she'd been on the phone talking about the date. I crept away without her knowing, saving the apology for another day. "Anybody in the mood for some chips and guac instead?"

DJ eyes me. "Fiesta again? What's with you and that place? They've got good food, but you've barely gone to Fishtail lately."

"I'm in the mood for the mole dip."

Caleb sighs. "You didn't."

He knows exactly why I'm going because I dragged him along with me last time. "We have to make sure that Rach isn't wasting her time. Plus, it's half off margarita night. We're basically saving money by going there instead."

DJ shakes his head, but Caleb pins me with a disapproving look. "You really need to lay off Rachel, dude. How far are you going to take this? You've sabotaged like three of her dates already."

Four, but who's counting? "Can you really sabotage something that was never going to work out to begin with?"

Caleb pinches his nose.

DJ snickers.

I grin. "So…" I press.

The running back sighs. "I guess I wouldn't mind a quesadilla. But you're paying for our drinks since I'm missing out on the ribeye."

"Deal."

Forty-five minutes later, we're sliding into a corner booth facing Rachel and some balding man with thick glasses wearing a sweater vest.

The waitress comes, and I order the mole dip.

Then, I send a passionfruit margarita to Rachel's table.

As soon as it's set in front of her, she stares at it before her eyes lift and search the room.

DJ and I lift our glasses.

Caleb grumbles under his breath.

Rachel shakes her head and shifts in her seat, trying to focus on her date with the nerdy-looking guy who probably works in IT somewhere and lives in his parents' basement.

But I see her peek in my direction every so often, and it's a small victory that swells my chest more than it probably should.

✪

IT'S HARD TO fathom that four years of college are almost up, which leaves a lot more questions than it does answers. Which is mostly why I'd skipped out on the original meeting I had with Rachel. I knew what she'd ask me, and I had no answer.

None.

Football was the biggest reason I went to college. Now...I don't know what comes next. More school? Work? She was the type of girl who had everything planned out. And I was the kind of guy who rarely knew what I was eating for breakfast the next morning.

It's a little embarrassing that I'm one of the few guys who have no clue what the future brings. Griffith has always known he wanted to go pro, and at the rate he's going, he'll be drafted in the fall. Caleb has been primed and ready to take over the family business, probably putting a ring on Raine's finger and popping a baby or two out to live the white picket fence dream. And DJ...well, since his shoulder injury, he's been talking about going to grad school as a backup option.

Maybe that's what I need too.

Approaching the door, I barely have time to say anything when Rachel says, "Come in and sit down, please."

She's using her authoritative voice, which I find hotter than I probably should. But it also means she's pissed.

I'm not surprised after showing up during her date. DJ and I may have indulged in one too many of the half off margaritas, got slightly tipsy, and tried sending random drinks to Rachel and her date's table until he told her he had to go.

He only paid half the bill like a loser, so I pulled the money out to cover hers and made sure the waitress got it before Rachel could pay.

"You don't have to thank me for dinner," I tell her light-heartedly, dropping into my usual seat in the chair rather than the couch we helped her maneuver in here. That was always Griff's spot, and it felt weird sitting where I was used to seeing him.

Rachel blinks slowly. "*Thank* you?"

"You're welcome," I beam, ignoring the incredulous tone she said it with.

She closes her eyes and lets out a sharp exhale. "Matt, that wasn't okay. How did you even know I was going to be there?"

How else? "I heard you."

Her eye twitches.

"You should really stop having personal conversations at work if you don't want people hearing them," I say, realizing quickly by the sharp glare she gives me that it wasn't a smart thing to say.

"Really, Matthew?"

Uh-oh. She pulled out the full first name. "I just think it's confusing, you know? Sometimes, it feels like you *want* me to know your plans."

Her gaping expression tells me I'm most likely wrong. "Why on earth would I want you to barge in on every date I have?"

Well, there are a lot of reasons. "Because they're not me," I answer honestly.

She's silent as she stares at me.

I shrug, leaning back. "You asked."

Slowly, she shakes her head. "You must think quite highly of yourself, Mr. Clearwater." She lowers her voice, eyes moving to the door before coming back to me. "We had one night together. That was all."

As casually as I can, I reply, "Sometimes, one night is all it takes."

Her eyes narrow, her glare like a dagger piercing my skin. But I'm not going to take it back if I mean it.

I pull out the folded piece of paper from my pocket, switching gears. "I filled out the application for my cap and gown like you requested all of us do. Are you still collecting the papers, or do you want me to turn it in myself?"

Her tongue drags across her bottom lip as she breathes through the obvious irritation she feels over this conversation. Begrudgingly, she murmurs, "I'll take it."

I set it on her desk and slide it over.

She puts it in a folder with the others. "I heard they're upping the number of tickets per person for each graduate from four to five, in case you wanted to invite one more person to watch you walk."

I drape an ankle over my bent knee. "Are you coming to watch us graduate?"

Us. Not me.

"I don't know."

"I can leave you a ticket."

She shakes her head. "You don't need to." She pulls up something on her computer. "Let's discuss next steps. You submitted your petition to graduate. Make sure you request the right ticket numbers. You can always ask for five even if you don't use them a—"

"What if I want you to have my fifth ticket?"

Rachel closes her eyes, mouthing something that looks like a countdown, before opening them. "I'm sure faculty will get the opportunity to go on their own accord." It sounds forced when she adds, "But thank you."

I'd like to think she's not going to be mad forever for the move I made, but I don't know what kind of grudges she's capable of. "I'm sorry," I tell her, gaining her focus back. "For overstepping during your date."

Surprise seems to widen her eyes a fraction.

I don't stop there. If I'm telling the truth, I'm going to tell her exactly how I feel. "I don't like that you're dating. And the guys you seem to be giving shots to look like tools who don't deserve an ounce of your time. But it's your time to do what you want with. I know I don't have a right to tell you what you can or can't do with them."

All she does is stare at me.

I scoot forward on the chair until I'm sitting on the edge, leaning my elbows on my knees and looking at her. "You're an amazing person, Rach. I always thought that. So, yeah. One night is sometimes all it takes. Pretty sure that's all it took for me."

Standing, I grab my bag from the floor and toss it over my shoulder as she continues to stare at me. Her cheeks are red, her lips parted like she's trying to figure out something to say.

I'm not going to be ashamed of anything I've said. It feels good to say it out loud. My chest feels lighter, knowing it's out in the open. "I think I'm going to look into grad school," I tell her, gesturing toward the computer. "If you need to put something in my file. I'll let you know what I decide for our last meeting."

Her mouth closes as she lowers her hands into her lap, a gentle nod all I'm greeted with.

"I'll see you later, Ruby Red."

CHAPTER NINE

Rachel

I T'S THE LAST game of the year for the Dragons, and they're six points away from tying with the Davis Stallions and going into overtime.

There are two and a half minutes left.

The Dragons get into formation.

Coach Pearce stands tense on the sidelines, arms crossed. The ball snaps back, and the clock starts.

Ricky Wallace, who was put under investigation for allegations made by multiple women on campus, runs the ball past two of his teammates who are wide open for passing, trying to dart past the Stallion's defense. They gain on him, one on either side.

"Throw the ball!" I hear someone sitting a few rows down from me yell in frustration.

"Pass it!" a couple of other onlookers echo as the clock counts down.

A minute.

Fifty-five seconds.

Fifty.

The defense lunges for Wallace, tackling him at the for-ty-seven-second mark.

"Dumbass," the older woman beside me grumbles, making it hard to keep a straight face.

Wallace is definitely that. After reading over his records, it was evident that he'd had more than one incident reported against him that inevitably ended up being struck out. The reports don't necessarily go away, but the repercussions do if the people filing them decide not to pursue them or the investigators decide there's no evidence to justify the consequences.

Something tells me it's a mixture of both because nobody with the number of strikes in his file should still be enrolled at Lindon, much less on the field.

Most of the Dragons go back to the sidelines, ignoring their quarterback on the ground. They're angry. I am too, and I'm not even on the field.

One player walks over and extends a hand.

Number eleven. Matthew Clearwater.

But Wallace slaps it away and gets up on his own, shouldering past the wide receiver who offered him an olive branch.

My eye twitches. I overheard Coach Pearce yelling at somebody over the phone about a drug test for Wallace the other day, and it was clear that he wasn't happy about it. It was also obvious that whoever was on the other end of the phone didn't care what the head coach wanted. Usually, random drug tests happen throughout the semester to make sure nobody is using and going against policies and scholarships. Lindon only has so much money to dole out to people, so they're strict with the rules.

Pearce knows that better than anybody, which I'm assuming is why he was fuming that day. I cringed when I heard him slam down the phone onto the receiver and cuss all the way down the hall until I didn't hear another peep.

I thought for sure that I'd see Ricky on the bench or absent completely, so it was a surprise when I saw his name and number jogging out onto the field with everybody else.

"Boys like that will never get far in life," the older woman beside me says with a shake of her head, pointing to Wallace as he makes crude hand gestures to the other team. "It's a real shame too. He's a decent player. He's just not a team player. That's what's gonna get him."

I turn to the white-haired woman with a small smile on my face. "You're not wrong," I agree sadly. "The old team played a lot better together. Since their captain's and wide receiver's injuries and their tight end leaving, it's been..."

"Painful," she finishes for me, sticking out her hand. "I'm Bea. I own the bakery on Main Street. I like coming to support the boys whenever I can break away since they practically live at my store off campus."

I've heard of the infamous Bea from Bea's Bakery. The boys spend a lot of time there. It's a busy place—popular with the college students for its good, cheap food and coffee. It's one of the reasons why I steer clear no matter how many invites I get from Matt or the others, even with the strong allure for her coffee that I hear nothing but good things about.

"I'm Rachel," I introduce, gently shaking her hand before pulling back. "I'm the athletic adviser for the team."

Her brows raise. "Ah. So you have the inside scoop. I almost feel sorry for you. I've seen how those boys act in my bakery. God help anybody who sees them in their element."

Cracking a tiny grin, I turn to the field where the team is standing around their coach. "They keep my life interesting."

"I have no doubt," Bea replies with a nod.

We sit in silence, save the mindless chatter coming from other bystanders waiting for the game to start again.

I lean closer to her and ask, "Do you think they'll tie?"

I have my own thoughts, but it seems like Bea knows plenty about what the Dragons are capable of. She's even wearing a red jersey with the college mascot on it. And if the boys are always at her place, she knows the play-by-plays I'm sure some of them talk about post-game.

"Honestly?" she asks.

I nod.

"No."

Lips rubbing together, I find myself bobbing my head in silent agreement. Maybe if they could pull together they'd have a better shot. But with Wallace running his own plays instead of doing whatever Pearce is telling him to, it's going to ruin their entire dynamic on the field.

"Yeah," I murmur. "I think you're right."

When the players jog back out, I hold my breath as they get into a new formation. There's one player in particular I watch closely.

Number eleven.

The ball snaps.

The clock starts.

It's a rush of loud cheering and anxious anticipation.

Forty seconds.

Thirty-five.

Thirty.

Twenty-five.

Twenty.

The Stallions intercept the ball, running it to the end zone and darting around the Dragons, trying to catch up to them.

Ten seconds.

Eight seconds.

Five.

Matt tries going after the ball as it flies through the air from one Stallion to the next but misses it by an inch.

With two seconds left, the Stallions make another touchdown, leaving the Dragons with a twelve-point loss as the clock hits zero.

I close my eyes as the opposing team starts celebrating their victory under the lights of our stadium.

"Well, there you have it," Bea says with a sigh. She pats my leg and stands. "There's always next season, right? Let's hope the players coming in can work together better than these guys."

I smile, because what else can I do? I feel bad for the boys who won't get a chance to prove themselves next year, but I'm glad that the younger players still have the opportunity. "I hope you're right."

"You should stop by the bakery sometime," she suggests. "I've never seen you there before, but I can tell you like coffee. I'm never wrong about those things."

I'm pretty sure caffeine is what really runs through my veins, so I crack a grin. "I don't think I'd function without it."

"Good. First one will be on me," she says, waving her

goodbyes and telling me she needs to head back to the bakery to make sure her granddaughter hasn't burned it down.

Ten minutes later, I'm waiting for the boys to leave the locker room. Fidgety, I tug on the custom jersey and shift my weight as a few of them start exiting, freshly showered and changed.

Most of them seem to be in good spirits despite the loss, which I'm glad. It's never fun ending a season this way. But Bea is right. Next season is another chance to make a difference, even if the OG boys I've gotten to know this year won't be coming back for it.

I wait another five minutes, hoping to catch Matt, when the locker room door opens, and the familiar face I'm looking for comes out.

Matt is laughing at something the person next to him says. They bump each other's fists and part ways, the soon-to-be graduate walking in my direction and waving at a couple of people lingering in the hall.

Before I can say anything, his eyes shift to my little hiding spot and land directly on the way my arms hug my torso.

He stops a foot away, looking behind him before wetting his lips. "You came."

"I wanted to support the team," I tell him.

His lips tilt up into a secretive smile when I lift my gaze. He does a once-over at my outfit. "I saw you in the stands and had to do a double take. You weren't in your normal spot."

My normal spot was in the middle of the stands, blended into the other football fanatics. By the time I arrived, the game was starting, so I crept into the section closest to the exit.

"Thank you," he says softly, tugging on the hem of my jersey. "For coming."

"I'm sorry you lost."

He rubs his lips together, releasing my jersey. "Me too, Ruby Red. Me too."

We stare at one another for a stretch of silence longer. "I wanted to see you before I left. I promised my sister I'd go back to Pennsylvania for the summer to spend time with her."

Matt's eyes follow my squirmy movements, from the way I rub my arm to how I move my weight from one foot to the other. "Are you planning on spending time with anyone else while you're there?"

Sadness sweeps over my chest at his hedging for information. "Matt…"

"It's just a question."

I look around at the people lingering in the hallway before my focus turns back to him. It's not just a question to him. "It doesn't matter if I am or not."

He stands taller, his right eye twitching. "It does to me."

"As a friend?" I ask quietly.

His nostrils flare. "Sure, Rach. As a friend."

I know what he wants me to say, but that can't happen. "You're still a student, and I'm still a faculty member. That isn't changing anytime soon, Matt."

"I'm graduating," he reminds me.

Throat bobbing, I nod. "I know. But then there's grad school. Our positions won't be any different than they are right now. That's why I wanted to say goodbye today."

His jaw grinds. "Goodbye." His Adam's apple bobs as he moves his head up and down slowly. "So you aren't coming to graduation to see us off? Even after everything you've been through with us?"

I've thought about it but haven't made up my mind yet. After Pearce heeded his warnings over involving myself in their lives, I'm not sure it'd be smart to. Then again, it wasn't smart to order pizza or cake and then go through a student's file either, so...

"I don't know yet," I answer.

A thoughtful noise comes from him as he looks away, evading my eyes.

"You should focus on being proud that you're graduating and enjoying your summer," I tell him, gently brushing his hand until he looks at me again. The hurt has grown on his face. "We both know you have plenty of girls who would love to have a shot with you."

"What if I don't want them?" he asks.

My touch lingers longer than it should, only breaking when I hear a throat clear from a few feet away.

Coach Pearce watches us, his eyes narrowed as they dart from me to Matt, to where my hand was moments before.

Face burning, I step back until there's a healthy distance between us. "Sorry again about the game."

As I walk away, I glance in Coach Pearce's direction. He's still watching me, but he simply shakes his head and disappears into the crowd without a word my way.

The next day, there's a singular ticket to the spring commencement taped to my office door. I don't need a note to figure out who left it there.

I stare at it for a long time.

It matters to me. His words have been ringing in my head since he said them.

Sighing, I slip the ticket into my purse.

★

GRADUATION AT LINDON University hasn't changed, so seeing the chairs set up feels like it did when I was walking across the stage in my red gown.

I'm supposed to be in my car on my way to Pennsylvania for a couple of weeks to be with my family for summer break. But the ticket that couldn't have weighed more than an ounce felt like cement in my purse wherever I took it.

It matters to me.

Tugging on the black dress that I haven't worn since my graduation, I feel an unease clawing at my stomach.

Following a group of people to the stands, I tuck a piece of curled hair behind my ear. I spent way too long getting ready for a graduation that isn't even mine.

As I head to a section of bleachers that looks relatively empty, I see Matt's family. Front and center, just like they are at his games. I offer them a wiggle of my fingers in greeting as I pass by, listening to them gushing over the boy who I'm here to see too.

"Hard to believe," the woman beside Matt's mother says. An aunt maybe? "Time flies by, doesn't it, Maureen?"

Matt's mom smiles. "It feels like he just came into our lives," she gushes, reaching for her husband's hand. "We're so lucky to have this. It felt impossible for so long, and now our baby is leaving us."

My mother was emotional during my high school graduation. Her face turned red, and it was hard for her to breathe. That night, she went to bed early and slept so long that Dad almost called 911. I thought she was being dramatic because she was going to miss me that much when I went to college, but I know now that wasn't it at all. Her disease had progressed more than any of us knew. Maybe even more than she knew.

Sitting down, I study the rest of the bleachers. I recognize quite a few families from their attendance at the big football games. I wave at a couple of them when they catch my eye before looking out to the field. I can see the peak of red coming from the tunnel where the players usually walk out of.

The back of my neck tingles, then I capture a glimpse of a faraway face.

Matt.

It's too far away to see him, but I know it's him. He's goofing off with a couple other guys, then starts dancing. And I know those moves. I've seen them on the sidelines and when he makes a touchdown.

"Rachel, right?" a familiar white-haired woman asks, stopping in front of me.

I look up and smile at Bea. "Hi. Are you here to support the Dragons too?"

I never went to the bakery like I said I would. Work got busy, and I'd been avoiding any places I knew Matt tended to gravitate. It was easier that way. "I come every year to show my support. Without the college, I wouldn't be in business."

"That's sweet."

She gestures to the spot beside me. "Mind if an old woman sits? My hip ain't what it used to be. I've been on my feet all day making sure my granddaughter would be set at the bakery so I could come here, and lord do I feel it now."

I scoot over. "Sit. Please."

She takes her time lowering down with a content sigh as soon as she's settled in. "You must be here for the boys too," she notes. "I haven't seen nearly as many faculty as I normally do at these things."

That probably has something to do with the emails we got from HR last week about an investigation against a few staff members in the athletic department. It led to Coach Pearce's abrupt exit only two days ago, followed by a few of the assistant coaches along with him. It's left a lot of tension at work, like any minute, the hammer could come down on me unless I'm careful.

Yet here you are, a pesky voice inside my head taunts.

Clearing my throat, I rub my arm and watch the students in the tunnel. "There's some turnover happening at the school, so you won't be seeing most of the football staff if that's who you mean. I think they were advised to skip this ceremony."

Her eyebrows go up with interest. "I've heard some rumblings around town but didn't know what was fact from fiction."

When someone as well-known as Pearce leaves the school after years of coaching, it's not going to go unnoticed. He's led the team to victory more than any other coach has in Lindon's history. Which is why the investigation against him has been so brutal. Zero tolerance is zero tolerance though. He let a lot of things slide to make sure they kept winning titles instead of disciplining the players, so it was bound to bite him in the butt eventually.

I'll admit, I'd been a little shocked when I saw him carrying out a couple of boxes with two campus police officers guiding him out. He passed me in the hall and said, "Good luck. You're going to need it," in a cool tone that had me stopping in my tracks and wondering exactly what he meant.

I was even more surprised when I got an email saying that Ricky Wallace was being expelled too, and that a new interim coach would be brought in for the fall unless they find a permanent replacement over the summer.

"I'm sure it'll get out soon," I tell Bea, not wanting to get into details. For all I know, I could come back from break and be told I have no position with the football team anymore either. They wanted to hire a new staff to get rid of the former corrupt one, and I wouldn't blame them if that included me with them.

My conscience has reminded me I deserve it.

One night or not.

And maybe...maybe it would be better that way. At least, that's what I've been telling myself to prepare for what *could* happen.

Bea studies the field. "I haven't seen you at the bakery yet," she notes casually. "The boys like to rift on Matt for it."

My eyes dart nervously over to her. It's not a suspicious accusation, simply a statement. Still, the caution buzzing under my skin has me repositioning in my seat. "Oh, well…" What am I supposed to say to that? "You know how they are. Always picking on each other about something."

The older woman hums, her cheeks twitching with a small smile. "And always about something important to them, it seems."

This time, I press my lips together and fight the heat rising under my skin.

It's smarter to say nothing at all.

Bea chuckles under her breath, patting my leg with her wrinkled hand. "I've seen it all in my day, child. Whatever it is that's got those shoulders tensing can't be that bad."

Matt used to say that Bea was the eyes and ears of Lindon, and I'm starting to see how true that is. "I don't know what you're talking about."

She smiles knowingly. "I'm sure. Tell me, child, who are *you* here to see?" When I can't produce an answer, her smile grows. "I've been around these boys for years. Watched each of them grow into their own person and deal with a lot of their own problems. But it always seems to work out how it's meant to in the long run. That's all I'll say about it. It's none of my business anyway."

Unable to comment, I manage to force a slow nod in acknowledgment. Matt and his friends love the woman beside me. They support her business and like her sass and banter. She's family to most of them. I can see why.

But that claw of discomfort only grips my insides ten times tighter as I think about what she said.

When the music starts, I know the ceremony is about to begin. I make myself focus on the students walking out in their formations to the rows of seating in the middle of the stadium rather than the woman who knows more than I'd like her to, humming thoughtfully to herself beside me.

The first half of the ceremony is a blur, but by the time they start calling out names, I perk up with anxiety. I don't know how to react, but when Matt's name is called into the microphone, and I see the six-foot-two football player stand, I can't help but cheer with the group of people in the section over.

And when he looks to the crowd, I can feel the way his eyes lock on me in the mix of people. Even though I'm sure he can't see, I offer a wave and thumbs up to show him that I'm proud of how far he's come. Because I am.

Despite how irritated I've gotten with him and how many boundaries the two of us have crossed, I'm happy for the graduate shaking hands with the line of people before joining his classmates back at their seats.

Bea laughs under her breath, gaining my attention when the next set of names is called to walk the stage. I turn to her, but she's watching the graduation with a big smile and a shake of her head.

A few minutes later, my phone buzzes.

Matt: *You came*

Me: *You invited me*

Matt: *Meet me by the locker room after this is over*

There's not a question about it. I could argue, but what's the point? I'll meet him, congratulate him, and go on my way. By this time tomorrow, I'll be drinking margaritas with my sister and trying to avoid Tatum and my father at all costs, so I might as well enjoy today while I can. Matt is someone I enjoy.

After the ceremony, I sneak out with the crowd and make a detour toward the locker rooms to meet the boy whose big day it is.

I think I beat him until two hands find my arm and tug me into an alcove and away from prying eyes.

Matt smirks at the startled noise I make, laughing when I swat him for scaring me. "I didn't mean to make you jump," he muses.

"You can't just grab a woman," I scold.

He grins. "Sue me."

I roll my eyes. "I can't sue you on your big day. Congratulations, by the way. How does it feel to finally be a graduate of Lindon University?"

All Matt does for a few long moments is look down at me. When his mouth lifts at the corners, I don't know what's on his mind until he says, "It feels like I finally have options."

I get that. Anyone in his position feels freedom right after getting handed a diploma. Until reality reminds you that life is about to set in. "Did you decide on grad school? The deposit is due soon if you're going in the fall."

He blows out a raspberry. "I don't want to talk about school right now."

I lean against the wall he's got me pinned against. "Oh. What do you want to talk about?"

"You came."

"I did."

He watches me, his eyes dancing with something that

brightens his face. "You look damn good in that dress, Rach."

I feel my cheeks heat. "It's old."

"It's hot."

Glancing down, I tug at the hem that feels a lot shorter than it did without his careful attention. "You're always the flirt, huh?"

"It's not against the rules anymore," he's quick to remind me. "After all, I'm no longer a student at Lindon. So, if I wanted to kiss you right now…"

My heart reacts to that by speeding up in my chest, and I worry he can see it trying to beat out of my skin.

He leans forward, almost teasing me with the possibility of a kiss. But instead of pressing his mouth against mine, he moves his lips to my ear. "And I think you'd like that."

I close my eyes, not wanting to admit that he may be right. Because it wouldn't be against the rules, which makes the temptation that much more intense.

Skin buzzing, I press my palms against my thighs. "I think you should go see your family before they start wondering where you are."

Matt leans back just enough to meet my eyes. They study me carefully. "You know what I really want to do?"

"What?"

"Kiss you."

"I know. You made that clear."

He shakes his head. "Not here. Not in secret where nobody can see us. Out there. In front of everybody. Friends. Family. Classmates. I wanted that moment of celebration where I can show the girl I like that I want her."

I swallow. Because...*damn*. Being wanted is one of the best feelings—like a buzz under my skin that sends prickles of heat up the back of my neck until I'm warm and fuzzy inside. But it doesn't feel like a feeling I can hold on to. "There are so many other girls who are better suited for you."

"They're boring."

"They're attainable," I correct, lips twitching downward. "And that bores you for some reason."

He doesn't give in. "Think what you want. But if I knew Caleb wasn't out there dropping on one knee to propose to Raine, I probably would have kissed the hell out of you and not given a single fuck about what anybody thought of it."

I blink. "Caleb is proposing?"

Matt sighs. "Is that all you heard? Come on, Ruby Red. It's not like that's shocking. You've been around Caleb. Man is dumbstruck in love with that girl. They're probably showing everybody the ring and planning a future with babies as we speak."

Then what is he doing in here? "Matt, go be with your friends. That's a huge deal, and I know how close all of you are."

"Are you leaving soon?" he asks, checking the time on his phone. "You said you were probably going to Pennsylvania for break."

I nod. "I leave in the morning."

"Give me tonight."

Oh, Matt. "Don't you have plans?"

"Sure," he answers, smirking. "With you. Nobody else I'd rather celebrate with. I've got a party with the family this weekend, so that clears me for a couple days. Come on. You can't feel guilty about anything. We're not doing anything wrong anymore. Say yes."

"You're going to grad school."

"But I'm not in it yet," he points out.

He's always going to have an argument.

"One night," he whispers, those lips only an inch away.

One night. I squeeze my thighs together when my mind takes me to all the possibilities that could happen in twelve hours.

Swallowing, I say, "We already had one night."

His eyes flare with mischief, which makes me nervous. "I'll make it worth it. I promise."

Matt reaches for my hand, squeezing it once before sliding his fingers leisurely up my arm until they stop below my chin. He tips my head up to meet his eyes, making me hold my breath for a moment so he doesn't see what he's doing to me.

My eyes dart to his mouth briefly before shooting back up to his eyes, earning me another knowing smirk from him as he begins to lower.

God. Can he hear my heart? I can. It's beating so hard in my chest that its wild thumps echo in my eardrums.

"One night," he whispers again, his lips only barely brushing mine when the door to the hallway bursts open.

I jerk back in time to see Caleb walking in with a distraught look on his face. When Matt sees him, he frowns.

"Cal?" he calls out.

"She said no," Caleb murmurs.

Matt and I share a confused expression before Matt walks

out of the alcove and over to where Caleb is leaning against the wall in his cap and gown. "What are you talking about? What's wrong, man?"

Caleb slides down the wall until he's sitting on the floor. When he looks up at Matt, there's a shadow over his face like he's not even here at all. "Raine said no."

My eyes widen.

Matt curses under his breath before glancing over his shoulder at me. Our moment is broken. Over. All I do is shake my head. His friend needs him right now.

I back away.

Matt watches.

I point to Caleb before turning the corner.

It's better this way.

Because one more night wouldn't have been enough.

CHAPTER TEN

Matt

THE GIRL SITTING across from me is hot. Blond. Big boobs. Lean figure. Everything I usually love looking at all wrapped up in a tight dress with bright red, enticing lips.

Except she's not Rachel.

She's funny. Charming. But she's not the brunette who I've been thinking about nonstop for the past month when I should be enjoying my summer away from school before I start my master's program in finance.

"…another one?" she asks, smiling at me.

I blink. "What?"

Her smile slips. "I asked if you want to get another round."

"Oh." I glance down at her empty glass that used to have a dirty margarita in it. It's not pink like the passionfruit kind that Rachel loves to drink. When did she finish drinking it? "We can if you want."

Brittany, an avid football fan who I'm fairly certain doesn't know anything about the sport at all, frowns. "You don't want to be here."

"What? No." I wince when her frown deepens. "I mean, no, it's not that. It's been a long day. I'm a little out of it."

And I can't stop thinking about another girl, but I'm

definitely not adding that part.

Her frown molds into a small smile. "I can think of a few ways to wake you up if you're interested."

Internally groaning at the suggestion that would normally make my dick twitch, I can't help but notice that it does nothing. There's no reaction. Not even a small nudge that says, *Hey, let me out for a test drive. It's been forever.*

And it has. At least forever for *me*. I hooked up with one person since my little drunken tryst with Rachel, and it was because of alcohol, testosterone, and a hint of desperation. When I realized she was going out with people, I figured it was time to stop obsessing. Didn't mean I was going to stop flirting, but I was determined not to be the type of guy who pined for someone who clearly didn't think I was worth it.

Except I didn't enjoy myself at all.

Not like I did with my former athletic adviser.

"As much as I want to," I tell my date, hoping to soften the rejection, "I can't. You're gorgeous, but I just don't think it's going to happen tonight."

Or any night, if I'm being honest.

The flirty expression on her face falls into one of irritation as she narrows her carefully painted eyes at me. "You're serious, aren't you?"

"Unfortunately," I mumble more to myself than her.

If the guys ever find out about this, I'll never hear the end of it. I'm the guy with a rep. A playboy with a don't-give-a-shit attitude. They're usually right.

For some reason, I can't go through with this though. "I'm sorry," I tell her, pulling my wallet out and sliding a couple of bills onto the table. "I can drive you home."

She pushes her chair back, collecting her bag with a disgruntled look on her face that twists those luscious lips downward. "Don't bother."

I watch as she flattens out her dress and saunters off, weaving through the crowd of people and out the door.

Swiping a hand down my face, I let out a long-winded sigh that relieves the pressure in my lungs. "Good going, Clearwater," I mumble to myself.

Sliding into my car in the parking lot, I pull out my phone and type out the name I have a million times on Facebook. It's a little pathetic actually, but I find myself curious about what the girl currently a state away is doing with her summer. And, more importantly, who she's doing it with.

Clicking on her name when I see her profile, my finger hovers over the "friend" button before scrolling down.

She was tagged in a few photos over the last few weeks. One with her sister Brie, who could be her clone in a slightly curvier body. One with a group of women that apparently were her sister's bridal party on some girl's trip to an amusement park. And...I frown, eye twitching when I see the picture of her sitting next to the same man from her sister's wedding.

She didn't tell me if she planned on enjoying her summer the way she told me to, but this might give me an answer.

Leaning back, I stare up at the ceiling of my car and think about what I want my summer to be like. I want to have fun. See my friends. Enjoy not being cooped up in classrooms or forced to do schoolwork. I don't have to worry about conditioning in August now that I'm done with undergrad, and I don't know how to feel about it.

A little sad.

A little relieved.

I have more time to myself before I begin graduate school, but I don't know what to do with it.

Despite everything I want to accomplish this summer, all I can think about is what Rachel is up to in Pennsylvania. And when I think about that photo of her and *Michael*, I wish I'd taken Brittany up on her offer after all.

Deciding not to stew in my own pity, I find DJ's name and type out a quick message, knowing he and Caleb are around.

Me: *Fishtail at 7?*

DJ: *I'm down. Drinks on u*

I roll my eyes.

Me: *Fine, but you get three max*

DJ: *Make it 4 and call me pretty and you have a deal Clearwater*

Me: *Drag Caleb along. He could use a few stiff ones*

After Caleb's failed marriage proposal, he's locked himself away and taken on ten times more work at his father's store. Something is going on with him that he hasn't shared, and I feel for him.

Hopefully, whatever it is can be fixed with a good buzz and a new girl to get under him so he can get over Raine.

✪

THE FORMER RUNNING back of the Lindon Dragons is somber as we sit in the back of Bea's Bakery. He hasn't touched his coffee or pastries that the sweet older woman gave to him for free after giving him a hug and saying, *"It'll be okay."*

He's barely spoken to anybody, trapped in his own thoughts. His own pain. "You should really eat something," I tell him, gesturing to the plate of pastries with my chin.

His throat bobs. "Not hungry."

"I know, man," I say. How could he be? If it were only a broken heart he was dealing with, I could be a lot more helpful. But when he told me and the guys that his father was diagnosed with brain cancer...Shit. What could you do? "But if you don't, your mom is going to worry about you."

That seems to get his attention, his distant brown eyes lifting up to meet mine. "You're right," he finally murmurs, reaching for the croissant and ripping it apart.

He still doesn't eat it after staring at the small piece in his hand, but it's a step in the right direction.

"Are you sure there's nothing I can do?" I ask for the fifth time in the past week since finding out the news. I feel helpless, and I hate it. Caleb is usually the voice of reason, the person we all go to when we need something. And he'll drop everything to give the shirt off his back to anybody who needs it. It's unfortunate that I can't do the same for him.

Caleb shakes his head, dropping the food back onto the plate. "No. There's nothing."

Silently, I nod. What else can I do but be here for when

he's ready? I'm surprised he even agreed to come out at all since he's been plastered to his father's side. His mother had given me a hug and thanked me when I picked him up, and I could tell she was worried for the boy who's clearly lost weight since things started going downhill.

We sit like that for another five minutes, other patrons coming and going to fill the quiet.

Saying that I'm sorry again won't get us anywhere. I am sorry. For him. For his mother. For his father. They're a tight-knit family—one that a lot of people in Lindon look up to. Nobody deserves what they're dealing with, least of all them.

He lifts his wrist and checks his watch. "I should probably get going. I told my dad I'd take care of the store before going to register for one of my summer classes."

My brows arch. "You sure that's a good idea?"

He pushes back to stand. "It's all I have right now, Matt."

I frown at the low tone of his voice. And how can I argue? The guy's dad has advanced cancer. His long-time girlfriend ended things. Who am I to say what he can or can't do to keep his mind busy?

Sighing, I nod once in understanding. "Just try not to push yourself too far, man."

He looks at me once, those eyes seeing me but not, before his chin dips in acknowledgment. Whether he'll listen or not is up in the air. I get it. He wants a distraction, and the store and school are going to be exactly that.

Even if it's not the best idea.

Caleb grabs my shoulder and squeezes once as he passes

me. "I'll try."

I watch him walk out with a deeper frown settled onto my face. He's like a ghost, floating around everybody and existing instead of living.

Bea shows up at my table only a minute or two later, her eyes going to the uneaten food. "We'll get through to him eventually," she tells me.

I stare at the door where he disappeared out of, hoping she's right. "I wish there was something I could do."

She pats my shoulder. "Be his friend. That's all you can do. We'll never know what it's like to be in his shoes, but we can be there for him as he deals with it."

When she walks away, there's only one person I can think of who knows what having a sick parent is like. I may not be able to understand, but Rachel can.

And Caleb needs somebody to relate to now more than ever.

CHAPTER ELEVEN

Rachel

TUGGING ON THE cross-halter neckline of the green dress, I look at myself in the mirror one last time before turning to my sister.

"You look beautiful," she says, beaming as she gives me an appreciative once-over. "And that dress makes your tits look bigger."

Her crudeness makes me snort. "Stop."

I do a double take in the mirror to see if she's right, and she is. The material does something to my chest, giving me a little extra lift and making them look perkier than usual.

"You know who would love it?" she asks, wiggling her brows in the reflection of the mirror at me. "Michael."

I knew she was going there the second those greenish-brown eyes flashed. "I don't see how he'd know what I look like in this dress, so I doubt it."

Brie considers that for the briefest moment before shrugging. "You two seemed to get along just fine at Callie's party the other week. It isn't a totally wild assumption to think you *may* see him again."

We did get along. Because I can be civil with anyone. It's not in my nature to be rude to someone, no matter the circumstances. Michael and I broke up and went our separate ways after high school, but that didn't mean I harbored any ill feelings toward him. It took me a while to accept that we wanted different things, and that was okay. I moved forward with my life just like he did.

"Callie even said it was like no time passed between you guys at all," she adds, clearly gauging my reaction.

Except she's not getting one. I do a little twirl in the flowy, shin-length dress and say, "Don't start letting your imagination run wild, Brie Cheese. There's nothing happening between me and Michael. Okay?"

"But—"

"No," I say, piercing her with a warning look over my shoulder. She's been on my case since Michael and I saw each other at her wedding this spring. Unbeknownst to me, he was a friend of Brie's husband Ryan. They met through his job, apparently. Whether Brie knew they were close enough for my ex to be invited to the wedding is beyond me. If she did, she definitely didn't tell me about it.

"Look, I'm happy for him. He's doing well in the police academy, and he's going to become a trooper like he's always wanted. That's great. Let me just work on myself and my career, too, without trying to mingle the past and the present."

My little sister frowns. "I just thought it might be nice for you to put yourself out there again and give him another shot."

"He lives here," I point out. "I don't."

"Are you planning on staying in New York forever?" she asks, her frown deepening at the possibility.

Swallowing, I stare down at my feet, wiggling my freshly

painted toes that Brie and I just got done at the salon an hour ago. "I don't know. It'll depend on what job opportunities I have in the future when I'm done with my master's program."

"And if you move back here…"

"If I move back here," I say pointedly, giving her a look. "Then I'll take it day by day. But Michael has always wanted to be a cop here, and I've always wanted…"

Well, more.

To get away.

To experience new places and people.

And when Mom died, to free myself from the constant reminder of the hole her absence left behind. Dad and Tatum only drove the desire to stay away. Far away. Even though I make time to call my father and catch up at least once every couple of weeks, it doesn't make being home easier. School was the perfect excuse to go away.

But I don't know what excuse I'll have for staying when I graduate.

Either way, I'm not making any promises to anyone. Not Brie. Not Dad. And certainly not Michael.

We talked during his cousin's birthday party a few weeks ago, catching up over the last six years that we didn't get a lot of time to do at Brie's wedding. It wasn't like anything significant was said, considering we both stayed friends online. I saw when he got into a new relationship and saw when it ended. He saw me go through undergrad and congratulated me on graduating. I saw when he got his associate degree and started working as a sheriff before leaving to join the state police academy. There wasn't much to talk about except cordial small talk that led to a few awkward moments of stretched-out silence.

"So, I guess a double date is out of the question?" she asks, sounding sadder than she should be for me.

She was never Michael's biggest fan, but also didn't hate him either. I'm not sure she ever really had a clear opinion on him. I liked it that way. In fact, I preferred it. But now, I'm just confused. "I don't get it. Why are you trying so hard to make this happen?"

Her shoulders slump. "I just want you to be happy."

I smile at her. "I am happy, sis."

"Really?"

I nod. "Really." *Or as happy as I can be.*

"And I guess I want a reason for you to come home," she admits quietly. "I miss you."

My heart does a funny little dance. "I miss you too, Brie Cheese. Every day. But Michael won't be the reason I move back to Pennsylvania. I'll never make a man the reason I go anywhere."

Her eyebrows go up. "You don't know that for sure. If you love somebody, you'd do anything for them."

"Then why couldn't they do the same for me?" I counter. "I'd rather they follow me for my dreams and future."

Brie offers me a small smile. "That doesn't happen very often," she says.

It doesn't. "I guess if the day ever came when somebody followed me to the ends of the earth, then I'd know it's really love."

My sister's expression softens. "I hope that happens for you then."

Me too, I answer in my head.

Brie's eyes go back to my boobs before she grabs hers. "Your tits make me want a boob job. How much do you think those are?"

I snort. "You were just bitching about how expensive cheese has gotten. I don't think fake boobs are in your future anytime soon."

She blows out a long sigh. "Dream killer."

I roll my eyes.

Then she asks, "Are you going to be at dinner with Dad and Tatum tonight?"

Internally, I wince. Because spending even two hours at the house I used to call home makes me feel itchy when I've been happily occupying Brie and Ryan's guest bedroom.

Suddenly, I wish we were still talking about Michael.

I glance at her chest to stall for an answer, since I haven't accepted our father's invitation yet. "You should do a consultation with a plastic surgeon to see how much it would cost."

She eyes me knowingly but doesn't call me out on the topic change.

I SHOULDN'T HAVE come. That's the first thing I thought when I stepped into the kitchen to see what was cooking. That's when I saw them. The walls.

They aren't yellow anymore. I've been staring at them for the last ten minutes, remembering how excited Mom was to paint them the pastel buttery color. Yellow was her favorite—it made her happy. I'd been five and tried helping her paint whatever I could reach. It was patchy and messy, but she didn't care. We listened to music and laughed and had fun the entire time.

Dad walks into the kitchen. "What is it?"

My nostrils flare when I take note of the ugly plaid curtains hanging from the window above the sink. "Mom loved the kitchen."

He's silent, flinching when he glances at the sage green where the original color used to be. "It was time for a change, kiddo."

A change.

"And whose idea was that?"

He doesn't need to answer for me to know.

Even the colorful lines and measurements drawn in permanent marker going up the doorway are painted over. Dad didn't even fight to have all the years of Mom marking our growth spurts before the first day of school to stay?

The last time I was here, nothing had changed except for Tatum's presence. I didn't love that, but it wasn't as gut-wrenching as this. Sure, there'd been some new throw pillows on the couch and a few new picture frames displayed around the house, but that seemed so minimal—easily ignorable.

She changed Mom's favorite room.

Erased her.

And Dad let her.

"Rachel..." Dad tries to say, before he must realize there's no point. I'm hurt, and he's the reason. What excuse could justify it? "It's hard for me too."

That's all he says.

Slowly, I move my head up and down. I'm sure it is hard slowly getting rid of any evidence of the person who lived here for decades.

Brie bursts through the door with Ryan in tow moments later. "I'm here, bitches!"

I look at Dad, then the walls.

Shaking my head, I walk out of the room.

Dad doesn't try to stop me and doesn't say anything the rest of the night.

I go back to Brie's house, missing my little apartment in Lindon ten times more when I'm closed into the small guest room, trapped in my thoughts.

That night, I get a message online from Matt's Facebook account.

Matt Clearwater: *Caleb needs you*

Matt Clearwater: *We all do*

I stare at those messages unblinkingly for what feels like forever.

It's a sign.

We all do.

I debate on accepting the message request before doing it, typing out a short response.

Rachel Holloway: *I'll be there tomorrow*

CHAPTER TWELVE

Matt

WHEN THE FIRST semester of grad school starts in the fall, it feels like I've been away for years instead of a few measly months. The campus doesn't feel nearly as fun as it did as an undergrad student, like a perpetual cloud is hovering over me everywhere I go.

The classes are no-nonsense and filled with ten times the reading I'm used to. The attendance policy is stricter. And I don't have football to let out any pent-up frustration.

I'm grateful that I still have a couple of friends who stuck around for grad school too—Caleb, despite all the reasons he probably should take a step back from school, and DJ. It's definitely not the same now that we don't share nearly as many classes together, or the football house since we're only allowed to stay if we're on the team. Walking the quad was a hell of a lot more fun when we had the swagger of saying we were a Dragon, and the apartment I share with DJ is lackluster and too small for parties.

Life now…sucks. There are no cheers from crowds watching Friday night football games to amp me up, or the buzzing of anticipation as the clock ticks down to the final seconds.

Walking into Bea's Bakery, I search the crowded space

until I spot DJ and his girlfriend Skylar in the corner. I nod my head in greeting when Skylar waves at me, nudging DJ, who has his head buried in a book. Probably another one that she convinced him to read. For the longest time, I didn't even know the guy *could* read. I always pictured him as the picture book kind of guy.

It isn't until I'm at the counter that I blink in surprise at the new hire working the register.

When Raine, Caleb's ex-girlfriend, sees me, she offers a stiff, shy smile. "Hi, Matt."

Had Caleb told me she worked at Bea's last time I saw him? I don't think so. Maybe he doesn't know. Or maybe he does, and that's why he told me and DJ in our group chat that he couldn't make it.

"Hey. Didn't know you worked here."

Her thumb jabs toward the back, where I'm assuming Bea is. "Bea knew I needed some money, so she offered to hire me based on my school schedule. It's been...interesting."

Elena comes out from the back carrying a fresh tray of chocolate chip cookies to replenish the display case. "In all fairness, you only mixed up three orders so far. And dumped one. And dropped that bagel on the floor and splattered cream cheese everywhere."

Raine winces. "Yeah. The *last* everything bagel that we had."

Elena shrugs. "The little girl got over it."

My best friend's ex frowns. "That's because Bea offered her two cookies to get her to stop crying."

Sounds like she's had a rough start. "If it makes you feel

any better, I just want a black coffee."

Elena perks up, nudging Raine. "See! That's an order you can't mess up."

Her chipperness makes me chuckle as Raine sighs. "Is that all?"

After paying and getting my coffee, I head over to where my friends sit. "You could have warned me," I tell them, sitting down.

DJ says, "We were as surprised as you."

"Not that it matters," Skylar pipes in.

One of my brows rises. "Shouldn't it? We're team Caleb. He was our friend first."

Skylar frowns. "Nobody is taking sides. Neither of them would ever ask us to."

All I can do is shrug, feeling loyalty toward the running back going through hell right now. He and Raine may have always been a package deal since high school, but I can't help but feel for the dude.

DJ switches subjects, sliding a plate of muffins over toward me. "Did you see the new interim coach that took over Pearce's job?"

I grab the one with blueberries in it, peeling back the cupcake wrapped from the bottom and splitting the muffin in two because I only eat the tops—aka the best part. DJ and I don't see each other much at the apartment because he spends a lot of his time staying at Skylar's dorm. "Yeah. I have no clue where they found him, but he looks like a dork."

Skylar says, "Be nice."

DJ looks at her. "Sorry, Blondie. But he's right. I popped

by the Sports Complex, and I swear the dude looked like he was going to piss himself when he saw some of the players."

I snort at that, shoving half the muffin top into my mouth and chewing. With a mouth still full, I say, "I'll give him this, a few of the fresh meat on the team look like they do 'roids."

The other former wide receiver nods, a small smirk curling half his hips. "I heard they're doing more drug tests after what happened last season with Wallace."

After DJ called in a tip that Wallace was using, he'd gotten drug tested. Since Pearce wasn't doing anything that took the egotistical quarterback off the field, DJ took it upon himself to get results. But it also put a lot of pressure on our former coach when allegations came out against Wallace that put Pearce in the hot seat for having ignored concerns about one of his players.

And now we have a new coaching staff, with a head coach that clearly has no idea what the fuck he's doing.

Before I can say more, Bea shows up out of nowhere and swats me upside the head. "Don't talk with your mouth full, boy. I know your mama taught you manners."

Christ. I swear Bea has eyes on the back of her head. "How did you do that?" I ask *after* swallowing my food.

Bea grins, refilling DJ's cup. "I know everything. I'm surprised you don't know that by now, after all this time."

DJ snickers, and even Skylar grins a little behind her drink.

Sighing, I lean back in my seat. "Have *you* seen the new football coach?"

The season has started, but I haven't made it to a game

yet. I'm not sure I ever will because I don't want my memories ruined by the new team or the life after the Dragons. I tried walking in once to see Rachel, but her office had been locked and dark, so I turned around and went about my day.

I haven't been back since, calling it a sign not to taint those memories I cherished now that my new life at Lindon hasn't compared.

I haven't even spoken to the brunette after telling her about Caleb. I know they talked, but I don't know if she got anywhere with him. He's still going to grad school and working at the store whenever he can. I see him around campus, but he's paler and skinnier than I'm used to. I'm not sure he's eating or sleeping the way he should, so I don't know if their heart-to-heart worked.

Bea gives me a look. "Give the man a chance. He's filling in for a person who left a lot of controversy behind."

Her chiding tone makes me reconsider. She's not wrong. Pearce was at Lindon for a long time. He left behind a legacy. A reputation. But he also left a lot of unsolved shit that the school had to investigate. Not ideal.

Bea lowers her voice to add, "But between us, I'm not optimistic we're going to see a full season this year. A damn shame."

Skylar frowns, and DJ and I share a look.

All I can hope is that this isn't the end for the Lindon Dragons. It would suck to go out that way after years of us building a name for the school. Now we went from news coverage about championship advancements to scandal.

"Maybe they'll find somebody better suited," DJ offers

optimistically.

"Hopefully soon," Bea agrees before heading over to refill coffee at the next table.

★

THE FIRST THING I notice when I see Rachel is how much bigger and doe-like her eyes are without glasses. Did she get contacts? LASIK?

Almost immediately after that observation, my eyes are drawn down to her bare legs shown off in the dress she's wearing. I never really considered myself a leg man before, but I could turn into one real quick.

Her head tips back as she laughs at something the tool in front of her says, and the sound is silky as it caresses my ears. But damn, do I hate that the new coach is able to make her sound that way.

Jealousy nips at my stomach, my nostrils flaring with irritation as I debate on turning around and going home or talking to her like I've been trying to do.

The new coach sees me before I can make up my mind, asking, "Can we help you?"

Rachel turns to see who he's talking to, standing taller when she sees me at the end of the hall.

I look between them for a second. "I was hoping to speak to Rachel." I don't bother with formalities, even though I should. And based on the tiny disapproving frown that weighs down Rachel's lips, she's not pleased.

The new coach, whose name I haven't even bothered to learn, dips his head and brushes Rachel's arm. "I'll talk to you later."

With that, he walks into what used to be Pearce's office and closes the door behind him.

As soon as it's just us, Rachel says, "What are you doing here?"

There's no "Hello" or "How are you?" from the girl whose frown settles onto her face.

Dumbly, I say, "You're not wearing glasses."

Her hands go to her face, brushing her cheekbones before dropping to the side. "I got contacts this summer."

"You look good." It's not meant to be flirty, but it makes her cheeks tint pink regardless.

Clearing her throat, she gestures toward the office. "Come on in," she says, her voice tight and professional.

It's as if we don't know each other—like I didn't ask her for help with Caleb or know what it feels like to be inside her. That's what she wants, though. To pretend.

Following her inside, I note that she leaves the door open. I don't make an effort to close it or point it out as she rounds her desk.

The couch is still where the guys and I left it, but there are a few new photos hanging. A potted plant is on her desk where the picture of her, her sister, and her mother used to be, and a few books have been added to the floating shelf on the wall behind her.

"You've redecorated," I note, scanning the pictures on the walls. There's one of her and her sister at her wedding and the old one from her desk beside it. There's another one further away, but the glare from the light makes it hard to tell who's in it with her.

Rachel sits, peeking at the pictures for a moment before nodding. "I wanted a little change." Before I can reply, she says, "You were rude to Coach Kelly."

I tell myself not to let the green monster prod at me just because she knows his name. They work together. It's not a shocking revelation. "I see you two are…friendly."

A passive look pinches her face. "Coach Kelly is nice. He's asked me to fill him in on the team. Stats. Past players. New ones. He's trying to make sure Lindon gets back to where they were."

I can appreciate that, but I don't like how chummy he was with her. "Just seemed like he knew you or something."

My fishing for information doesn't go over her head. "We've had a couple of meetings. We've talked. He's a good guy. Now, is there a reason you're here?"

"We haven't spoken," I point out.

"We don't have a reason to, Matt."

I wish that didn't tighten my chest as much as it does. "I just…" I look back at the pictures hanging on her walls before expelling a breath. "It's weird. Being here on campus and not being *here*. Not playing. Not being in this office for check-ins. Everything is different."

Her expression softens. "That's natural. You'll adjust. It's only been a month. By the end of the term, you'll be used to your new routine."

Will I? "I don't know what I expected," I tell her, thinking about the homework I'm already buried in. "Classes suck way worse than they did before. There's more work and no reward."

She offers me a sympathetic smile. "You miss football,"

she states in understanding.

Silently, I nod.

Rachel watches me fidget in my chair. "You could always come to games. I know it's not the same, but you can still be part of the Dragon family."

My lips twitch. Watching the game from the bleachers is as bad as watching it from the bench. It's about the adrenaline, the rush when the crowd goes wild when we score. I'll never get that back.

"It's not the same," I murmur defeatedly.

I'm not quite sure why I came here. There's nothing Rachel can do—no way for her to make me feel better. Life moved on the way it always does. I graduated. Stopped playing football. And got tossed into the next phase of life.

And I...I hate it.

"Maybe this was a mistake," I say, more to myself than her.

"What?"

I gesture around us. "This. Applying for grad school. Not trying harder to make football my career path the way Griffith did. It's not like I suffered any bad injury like DJ. If I really trained, I could have at least given it my all to make it to the big league. I missed my opportunity."

For a moment, Rachel is quiet. Contemplative. I can tell she feels bad, which isn't what I want. I don't need her pity. I just need...What the hell *do* I need?

"You never talked about that as a possibility during any of our meetings," she notes.

What was the point? "You met me during my senior year. Maybe if I hadn't fucked off for the three before that, I could have had a better chance at making something of myself."

Rachel's lips twitch downward. "You have the chance to make something of yourself every day, Matt. That didn't end just because you chose not to work toward a pro football career."

I lift a shoulder, not wanting to believe she's right because I'm in too bitter of a mood to accept that she is.

"You're going through a lot of changes," she says gently. "I'm sure it's bringing up a lot of what-ifs for you. But that's no way to live your life. Trust me."

I look at her. "Sounds like you're speaking from personal experience."

She goes to answer, then stops herself. Her eyes glaze slightly, becoming distant and muting the color I've grown to like so much. Typically, she only looks that way when it's about her mom.

"You can tell me," I say.

Leaning back in her chair, she glances at the picture on the wall again of her with her sister and mother. "My mom…" Her voice is thick, forcing her to clear it. "My mom was an elementary school teacher for the longest time before switching to middle school. She loved the job—loved teaching and the kids. It made her happy. Ever since I was little, I told her I wanted to be one too. She'd even buy me school supplies to use so I could line up my dolls and stuffed animals to teach lessons to in my bedroom."

A nostalgic smile tilts her lips. "Going into education was all I planned for myself because of her. And I know it meant ten times more to her when she got sick and had no choice but to leave the job she loved so much. Making her happy, making her proud, was what I cared about most when she had very little else to look forward to."

That smile turns watery. "Do you regret studying to become a teacher?"

Rachel doesn't answer right away. "There were other things I considered, but all within the realm of education. I'm here." She lifts her gaze to meet mine. "Becoming an adjunct professor or counselor would make me happier than teaching in a different setting, so I'm weighing some options. It's the best of both worlds. One she and I could both be happy with."

She's still trying to make her mother happy.

"But are *you* happy?" I ask, seeing a dullness in her eyes that makes her face dim.

All she says is, "I have no reason not to be."

That's not an answer. Not an honest one, anyway. "My parents were afraid I'd get hurt if I tried going pro," I admit, stretching my legs out in front of me. "Not only physically, but mentally. Probably emotionally. They've always supported me, but they knew it was a tough road to go down if I wanted to make it to the NFL someday. They were worried I'd overdo it."

"Is that why you didn't pursue it?"

I've never let myself think about it much. "I think it's the biggest reason."

Self-doubt definitely played a part too. I've never been the strongest player or the fastest one. For a while, I struggled in the team setting because I wanted my time to shine. That doesn't work if you want to make it to the top.

"I had a little too many faults to get where I wanted to

be," I admit, shrugging again. "And I think I wanted to make my parents proud of me in other ways. By getting a stable job and doing well in life. But now that I'm here…"

She's right. It's an adjustment. I can't spend hours goofing off with the boys and burning off energy at the same time. There are no more drills. No more film footage. Nothing I'm used to.

I guess it's common to want to make people proud, but it's hard not to beat yourself up over the things you wish you could have done differently.

"You want to know my biggest regret?" I ask her, unafraid to lock eyes. She doesn't answer, so I tell her anyway. "If I hadn't gone to grad school, I wouldn't have had to sacrifice *this*."

I see her throat bob with a swallow, her response simply to gape at my honesty.

But it's true.

I wish she would have given me a night the day I graduated instead of leaving for Pennsylvania. I wish I never would have sent in my deposit for my spot in my master's program.

Simply put, I wish things were different.

Eventually, her raspy voice says, "Don't."

Don't. Don't what? Be honest? Admit my feelings? Don't like her? Don't think about what could have been? If only it were that easy.

"I know, I know." I stand, looking down at where she remains behind her desk. "I'm a student. You're faculty."

She draws her bottom lip into her mouth.

"But you know what, Rach?"

She still stares.

"We both deserve to be happy too."

CHAPTER THIRTEEN

Rachel

HALLOWEEN FEELS DIFFERENT without the silly pranks the former players used to pull on each other, and the fun decorations they'd go all out putting up in the hallways and offices. I swear, I still find fake cobwebs in my office from last year.

I've only seen a couple of the players wearing goofy costumes since getting here a few hours ago to start one-on-one meetings with the team. One of the starting wide receivers was dressed in a cardboard box made to look like a nightstand with a sign that said, "Your favorite one-night stand," which made me laugh and roll my eyes. The quarterback who replaced Ricky Wallace was in a dragon pajama onesie representing Lindon's mascot. And one of the running backs just wore his uniform all day.

I remember my first Halloween with the Dragons. Everybody dressed up. Some of them went all out more than others, and they asked me to judge them on the top three. Except, whoever won had to buy everybody pizza and wings instead of the other way around. I'd felt bad when I decided Daniel won after stapling various shades of gray paint samples to his shirt and saying he was *Fifty Shades of Gray*.

As I'm preparing for Dean Avery, the team's tight end, to

come in for my last meeting of the day, I can't help but think about the last two months.

When Matt saw me at the start of the semester, I understood where he was coming from. Not seeing the team had been foreign—almost disappointing. I'd gotten used to their antics. They were charming and harmless—well, mostly harmless—and I enjoyed their company.

The new team keeps to themselves. Maybe they were asked to after everything that's happened over the last few months. Lindon doesn't want any more drama, and I get it. The number of emails I've gotten from HR reminding me of the rules has been plenty of reason to try keeping to myself too.

Still, seeing the defeated look on Matt's face makes me feel bad for withdrawing. I've seen him around campus, and he hasn't looked much better. I can tell there's a weight on his shoulders that I feel a little blame for.

But what can I do? Nothing. Especially not what I'm sure he'd love for me to do, which crosses a lot of the ethical lines that HR has been highlighting in their emails to Lindon staff about very much not stepping over.

Lately, it's felt like I've been failing a lot of people. Caleb would barely talk to me about his father. Everything is so fresh and chaotic for his family right now, so I don't blame him. They're trying to help his dad by making him as comfortable as they can. The best I could do was tell him I would be available anytime he needed to talk because I knew what it was like from coping with my mother's illness. He thanked me, and I haven't heard from him since. I'm not going to push or pressure him. He's still absorbing what time he has left with his family, and I know firsthand how important that is.

And Matt's predicament...well, I wonder if I could have pointed him in a different direction. One he would have been happier pursuing. I know he loved playing, but I didn't think he ever considered it a long-term dream. He'd always been so unserious whenever we met—focused more on flirting than planning ahead. If I'd known he felt otherwise, I could have tried harder to push him in a different direction so he wasn't stuck somewhere he wasn't happy.

His parting words echo in my head, and I decide to push them far, far away. Because we do deserve to be happy, but I know I can't be the person who makes him that.

Not right now anyway.

The thought gets interrupted by a harsh knock on the door before Dean appears at my doorway looking less than pleased being here. I'm not sure I've ever seen the twenty-year-old smile once since meeting him in September.

"Hi, Dean," I greet. "Come in."

The sophomore grunts as he walks in, dropping into the seat and staring at the floor.

One thing is for sure.

I'm determined not to fail this team.

I SEE THE scowl from across the quad. Pinpoint it with a worried frown, even with the tens or twenties of other faces going to various buildings for classes. Matt usually doesn't look that way unless something, or someone, got under his skin.

The last thing I should do is head over there, but my feet don't seem to get the message.

Veering off the path that will take me to the Sports Complex where I'm supposed to have a meeting with Coach Kelly about a few of the Dragons struggling to keep up their GPAs despite my best efforts to help, I head directly toward the former wide receiver whose face is shadowed over.

As if he senses me, he lifts his gaze and turns it a fraction until we lock eyes. I stop a few feet away, moving off to the side, when a group of girls pass by. I notice how one of them gives Matt an appreciative once-over, making my eyebrow twitch.

"What's wrong?" I ask, cutting right to the chase. I'm sure we both have places to be, so I don't want to hold him hostage. Especially since the mid-November weather has made the temperature drop to uncomfortable digits, making the air prick my face.

He evades my eyes, rubbing his lips together like he doesn't want to tell me.

"Matt," I say softly, taking another step closer. "You can talk to me."

His instant response is, "Can I?"

Flinching at his tone, I stifle a sigh. I guess I deserved that, huh? I've been avoiding him, and he's reluctantly respected the space I've put between us. "Yes, you can. I know I haven't made it easy, but…"

It's for the best, is what I want to say. But I don't. Because his scowl deepens, carving his face with irritation.

No. He doesn't need me to say that. He already knows.

I shiver when I'm hit with a chilly breeze, watching as a few more leaves fall off the trees that become even more naked as each day passes. I've always struggled this time of year. I was built for sunshine and warmth, not clouds and cold. Fall is pretty here in Lindon, but it's also a reminder of what's to come for the next six months.

Eventually, Matt huffs out a sigh. "If I don't pass my midterm in Gomez's class, I'm screwed."

Understanding has me nodding. "Okay. That's not the end of the world, right? You just need to do a little more studying. How bad can your grade be?"

The look he shoots me tells me all I need to know. Pretty bad.

Popping my lips, I try being the glass-half-full type of person. "Midterms don't start until next week. That gives you plenty of time. Maybe you can make flashcards like you've done in the past. Those seemed to work for you."

Resignation drops his shoulders. "But I also had people to study with. I can't do it on my own. You know how distracted I get."

He does. There were a few times I wanted to rip my hair out whenever his undiagnosed ADD would make him focus on anything but the task he needed to get done.

"There's the tutoring cen—"

"No way. Only nerds go there."

I wince at his judgmental comment. And, okay, maybe I was a tiny bit offended. Because *I* used to go there my sophomore year of undergrad when my math class was kicking my butt. Basic math I'm fine with. But anything other than that is a struggle I hate admitting.

"Matt, I'm trying here." He's not making it easy to give him suggestions.

When those gray-blue eyes lock on mine, I know they're pleading for silent help. He's stressed. More than he usually is. I know grad school hasn't been what he expected, and part of me still feels slightly guilty for that.

So…"I don't have a lot of free time this semester," I tell him. I graduate with my master's degree in the spring, so the workload has been gruesome. Between that and the team, my free time is limited. I don't mind it. I like keeping busy. But it means not having much of a personal life outside of Lindon. "But I'm sure we could find a couple days this week to study together."

Matt perks up. "You'll help me?"

"I'm only going to help you study, Matt."

The warning look I give him probably doesn't do much, but he nods anyway with a new shine of hope in his eyes. "You're the best, Rach."

I look at my smartwatch, trying to hide the concerned expression weighing down my lips. I really hope I don't regret this. "I need to get going, but stop by my office tomorrow at six. We can work on the flashcards and set up another day to go over them a few times."

"I'll bring us food."

"You don't have to—"

He's already walking away. "I'll see you tomorrow at six."

And, thankfully, he does.

The next night, he shows up at 5:59, holding a paper bag with Fiesta's logo on it. It smells delicious, especially since I hadn't had time to eat more than a slightly stale granola bar that I found in my purse.

He lifts it with a wink. "I hear the mole dip is good, so I got extra."

Sighing, I push off the flirting. "Let's get started, okay?"

He sits down and pulls out his notebook, setting it on my desk next to the food. "Anything for you, Ruby Red."

Maybe it's a sign I should put a boundary up—draw a line and make sure he doesn't cross it. Because the next night, he comes back to my office at six p.m. on the dot with a brown bag full of subs. An Italian for him, and a chipotle chicken for me. I stare at the order I used to get every time I went to the local sandwich shop and remember when he crashed another date I had there.

He remembered at least a third of the material we put on the cards and went back and forth on for an hour and a half.

The night after that, he brings a small pizza to share from Dante's, the pizzeria in town that I used to go to with the Dragons to celebrate their victories. I haven't been since the night he came back with me to my apartment, and the food tasted nostalgic in my mouth. It also distracts me as I remember what preceded the celebration. After two hours, the food is gone, and he remembers almost all the flash cards.

A day before his exam, he brings coffee and doughnuts from Bea's Bakery. We go back and forth for an hour and forty-five minutes until he gets every single card right. We high-five, then he hugs me and thanks me for helping him. That hug is the closest I've let him get since the day he graduated.

Because I don't trust myself or the gentle buzz that is always there, settled under my skin, wanting more.

The day before Thanksgiving break, there's an exam taped to my office door, with a B plus circled in red permanent marker at the top. I know whose it is before seeing Matt's name written in the corner.

I smile to myself.

When I peel the exam off the door, a Post-it note flutters to the ground. Bending down to pick it up, I recognize the chicken scratch scrawled across it. Well, the numbers written.

A phone number.

No name.

There doesn't need to be.

What I should do is put it in the trash, not in my bag. But that's what I do. And not only do I put it safely in my purse, but I tuck it into the only internal pocket there is with a zipper, where I usually keep extra cash, or my credit card, or sometimes a tampon. The important stuff.

I think about it the rest of the day, even when Coach Kelly comes in and asks me if I have plans for dinner since I don't have any more meetings on my work calendar.

"I've noticed how busy you've been," he says, leaning in the doorframe. "All those extra meetings at night you've had must make it hard to have dinner."

He's usually not around when Matt is, but he's noticed. Cement settles into my gut. "I manage," I tell him, smile wavering.

"Let's go out to dinner," he says. "Celebrate all you've accomplished."

Coach Kelly is nice. Attractive. There's no reason *not* to tell him yes. But I do.

"I can't," I lie and tell him I have a lot to catch up on at home before seeing my family for Thanksgiving. I'm already packed, and my car is full of gas.

But the less he knows, the better.

"I'm sorry."

And I am.

That little voice in my head tells me to change my mind. *Say you'll go*, it prods, poking me with its invisible finger until guilt creeps into my stomach when I see the shy smile the interim coach offers me after my rejection.

I don't accept the offer.

I thank him for it.

Tell him another day.

But, deep down, I don't think that day will come. And I tell myself there's a hundred reasons why, but they're all bullshit. Because I know it has everything to do with the number inside my purse from the boy who shouldn't be in the back of my mind.

CHAPTER FOURTEEN

Rachel

THERE'S SOMETHING POKING my cheek, stirring me from the much-needed sleep I fell into only a few hours ago based on the time on the alarm clock when I groggily peel one eyelid open.

"Pssst," someone whispers, jabbing me.

Mumbling incoherently, I swat them away.

"Pssssssst."

Grabbing the other pillow that smells freshly of lavender laundry detergent, I cover my face with it and turn onto my side, hoping the intruder will go away.

"Pssssssssssssssst."

"Oh my God," I groan tiredly, getting the pillow taken away from me.

When I peel both eyes open, I see my sister's bubbly face peering over me. "Oh, good," she says, the hazel-green eyes we share bright with unabashed mischief. "You're awake."

I blink past the bright light streaming through the window, suddenly remembering where I am when I see the pale blue walls covered in forgotten boy band posters I used to obsess over as a teenager.

When my eyes finally adjust to the sunlight beaming in through the open white curtains, I look to the girl who looks so much like me and Mom. Same round, soft face, warm features, and button nose. "How could I not be when you're stabbing me with those claws?"

Brie stares at her pointy brown nails with pumpkins and leaf designs covering a few fingers. "They aren't as long as they used to be. I'm getting used to them being shorter."

That's not like her. She's always prided herself on having long, polished nails with extravagant designs that she spends way too much money on at the salon. "Why?"

Her top teeth bite down into her bottom lip to fight a growing smile. "Well..." Her mouth grows into a bigger smile, making my brows pinch the longer she stares at me with an excited expression.

Grumbling, I rub my tired eyes. I got up early to beat traffic. I didn't sleep well since I had no idea what I was walking into. Dad and I have barely spoken over the past couple of months. Every time he tried, our phone calls became stretched out with awkward silence. I never ask about Tatum, and anytime he brings her up, I shut down. It didn't make me excited to come home, even if I was looking forward to a home-cooked meal.

"Is there a reason you felt the need to wake me up at..." I glance at the alarm clock again and sigh internally. I've barely slept for two hours. "Noon? I thought I asked Dad to let me sleep until at least two. He said dinner wasn't going to be until six anyway."

"It's the afternoon. You should be up by now. You're the morning person out of the two of us."

Usually, that's right, but I only got a couple hours of sleep last night. Dropping my head onto my pillow, I blow out a raspberry. "Not today I'm not. Plus, it's Thanksgiving. I should be allowed to be lazy."

She repositions on the bed, using my blanket to cover her legs. "I can't wait any longer. I wanted to tell you sooner, but we had to make sure the home tests were right."

My brain is still slowly waking up, so I'm not understanding what she's saying as I repeat her words in my head. "Brie, what are you—" I stop myself when it clicks, sitting up quickly with wide eyes. *Home tests.* "You're not."

She nods, giving me a white, toothy smile.

"Oh my God." My gaze goes to her flat belly, which she starts caressing lovingly.

My sister is pregnant.

Brie beams when I look back up at her. "I made Ryan drive us here early so I could tell you first. He's helping Dad make the green bean casserole downstairs."

I don't bother pointing out that none of us like that casserole because her news is far bigger than the fact Tatum has messed up our holiday tradition again by adding new side dishes and trying to take our old ones out.

"I'm the first one you've told?"

Her head bobs enthusiastically. "There's nobody I'd rather tell first. You've been the one in my corner our whole lives. Even when we disagree about...stuff."

Stuff. People. Same difference.

"Brie..." Words are beyond me. I lean forward and wrap her in a tight hug. "Congrats, sis. I'm so happy for you."

She hugs me back, squeezing me the same way I am her. "Ryan and I went to the hospital a while back," she admits quietly, peeling away and nibbling her lip. "To do the genetic testing. We wanted to see if I was a carrier for Huntington's like Mom was before we started trying. You know, just in case."

Why didn't she tell me? "When did you do that? I could have come with you. We could have done it together like we talked about after Mom..."

Sheepishness coats her face. "I was going to ask, but you've been so hesitant to come home. I figured if I asked, you'd make an excuse not to."

I know I haven't been Dad's or Tatum's number one fan, but that wouldn't have stopped me from finding time to support my sister. "I'd do anything for you, Brie Cheese. You should know that by now."

Her eyes flicker down. "You didn't stay for me. You used to promise you wouldn't leave like Mom did."

She'd begged me not to go back to Lindon after Mom passed and cried when I told her I was going to attend grad school there. I never wanted to see her look that way again, knowing I did it to her. Deep down, I know it was selfish to leave because of Dad and the memories surrounding me here when Brie was going through the same thing.

But I still left.

Chest aching, I grab her hand. "I'll never leave like Mom did. I never want you to think you can't call me about this sort of stuff. We always said we'd get tested together if we decided to go through with it."

She nods. "I know, but..." A tiny sigh escapes her lips. "You've had more important things to focus on. You're busy with school and work. I want you to be happy, and I know being here is hard for you."

Guilt wraps its claws around my heart and pierces it. "I'm sorry, Brie. I've been pretty selfish, huh?"

She shakes her head. "You've been living your life. It's no different than what we're doing here, right?"

I guess. I look at her stomach again. "I still can't believe you're pregnant. So, the tests you did at the hospital were...?"

"I'm not a carrier," she confirms with a warm smile. "It was pretty scary. Once we found out, we decided to go for it. I'm actually further along than I thought because the last couple of periods I had weren't actually my cycle. I guess it happens to people. If it weren't for the horrible back pain that led me to the doctor's, I probably would have wound up on that show *I Didn't Know I Was Pregnant*. It seemed wild to me that women wouldn't know something like that, but then I took eight different tests after getting home from the doctors to make sure they weren't lying to me."

I laugh. "Why would they lie to you about something like that? It's their job to tell you these things."

"They could have accidentally switched my pee out for somebody else's," she theorizes. "Or switched my file with the person next door. Crazier things have happened. Did you hear about the surgeon who accidentally took out the wrong organ from his patient and killed him? Because, apparently, that happens sometimes."

I didn't hear about that. "That's...bad."

"For all I know, I could have a doctor like that who obviously doesn't know how to read. Negative could look positive to them."

I roll my eyes. "How far along are you?"

"Four months."

My eyes widen. I'm starting to see why she could have been a valid candidate for the next season of that show. "Wow, that's..." All I can do is soak that in for a minute, taking in how much she glows. "I'm going to be an aunt."

Her head bobs. "Worth being woken up for? Or...?"

I laugh, hugging her again. "I guess so."

Her arms wrap around me and squeeze tightly. "Did I mention that there's food? Ryan and I made candied yams since you made them last Thanksgiving. And we brought the ingredients for the stuffing to do later."

"The stuffing is already done," a new voice says from the doorway, breaking us apart.

Brie and I turn to her husband, who's in his typical jeans and plaid shirt combo. If I went through their closet at home, I'd find multiple pieces of the same thing.

"Hey, Ryan," I greet.

Brie frowns. "You made the stuffing? I thought we were going to do it with Rachel."

Her husband jabs his thumb behind him toward the stairs. "I told that to your dad and Tatum, but she insisted that she'd make it to let Rach sleep longer."

Ryan welcomes himself into my childhood bedroom, looking around at the décor that's barely changed over the years.

My sister and I exchange a look, her frown deepening when she hears that Dad's girlfriend took it upon herself to make the sacred recipe. The last time she insisted on making one of the side dishes we'd perfected for years, she didn't do it right. When we pointed it out, Dad scolded us for being rude. But he knows I hate raisins in the stuffing. When I pointed that out, he simply told me to pick them out.

"Your dad was helping her with it," he reassures knowingly when he catches a glimpse of our worried expressions. "I'm sure it'll be fine."

Stretching, I wince when my shoulder pops and settles back into its socket. "If you're not letting me go back to sleep, can we at least go downstairs so I can be properly caffeinated?"

Ryan helps Brie slide off the bed, winding a supportive arm around her back until she gets her footing as if she's already nine months pregnant.

He's going to be a good dad.

"Tatum already has a pot going," Brie tells me. "She knows how much you love your caffeine, so she made a fresh one."

I try not to make a face. I was able to avoid Tatum this morning by arriving late, thanks to a bad pileup on I-81. It hadn't been an intentional move, although I'm sure she thinks it was deliberate since she told Dad after I left over the summer that she felt awkward the entire time we'd had dinner, thanks to the weird lulls in conversation.

Tossing the comforter off me, I follow Ryan and Brie to the staircase, where I hear laughter echoing from the kitchen below.

Brie links our elbows together. "Are you okay?" she asks quietly.

I glance at the old family photographs still hanging on the walls and knock my shoulder against hers. "Yeah, I'm fine. Being back here feels weird, is all. Dad and I never really resolved anything from last time."

Her eyes go to the closest family picture of us with Mom and Dad all posing in color-coordinated outfits that Mom chose. It was fall, so she opted for maroon sweaters that itched and made Brie and me wear matching braided hairstyles. At the time, I thought it was dumb. But now I'd do anything to do another set of pictures with her. Matching outfits and all.

Ryan turns to look over his shoulder. "It's only as weird as you make it."

Brie tugs on my arm. "He's right, you know. I think we're going to have a lot of fun while we're here. And if you need me to pretend like I know about the boy you're madly in love with at Lindon to get Dad and Tatum off your back about themselves, then I'm game."

My heart drops at the thought of Matt. "Boy?"

She shrugs. "Yeah. Your fictional boyfriend. We can make something up as we go."

I give her a long look, feeling only slightly relieved. "I'm good, but thanks."

Brie giggles. "I'm just saying, it could be fun. I did go to theater camp that one summer. I learned some things. But if you want to be all honest and boring, that's fine too. It's probably better they don't think you've got someone, or they'll grill you about where he is and why he's not here with you."

Snorting, I say, "Says the girl who's been pressing me to get laid before my vagina shrivels up forever."

"That's an interesting conversation to walk into," Tatum says next to my red-faced father beside her.

Both Brie and my brother-in-law start laughing when my face turns a similar shade of red as Dad's. "Er, sorry, Dad. We were just talking about...Never mind."

After a moment of pause where all of them are watching me, it's Tatum who says, "We have some leftover breakfast if you're hungry, Rachel."

Ryan and Brie go into the dining room after Tatum walks into the kitchen to grab the dishes and silverware, leaving only Dad and me by the staircase.

"Sorry I was late," I tell him. "That accident on 81 caused standstill traffic for over an hour, and I already had a late start to my drive. I thought I'd be here earlier."

Dad shakes his head. "Don't worry about it, kiddo. We're glad you made it safe. The news was covering the accident this morning. I guess there was black ice from the temperature drop. Thankfully, there were no fatalities, but someone did need to be airlifted. It was better you kept it easy."

Brie's laughter has us both turning to the dining room, where she and Ryan are looking at something on her phone.

I wrap an arm around Dad's waist and rest my cheek against his shoulder. "I'm excited to be here and eat food I don't have to make, order, or microwave. Even if Brie wakes me up like she used to when we were little."

He chuckles, winding his arm around me and hugging me into him. "I tried getting her to leave you be, but you know how she gets."

Nodding at the familiar reply, I let out a soft laugh. "I wouldn't have wanted to get in her way right now. I heard what she almost did to Ryan's coworker at their Fourth of

July party."

From the dining room, Brie says, "He asked if I gained weight! I was bloated. That ass is lucky I didn't tackle him. He would have snapped like a glowstick."

Ryan snorts, Dad chuckles, and I shake my head. "Then you probably would have been arrested for assault, sis," I point out, walking with Dad to join them at the table.

Brie waves me off. "If you saw the police force they have here now, you'd know they wouldn't arrest me. They all know me."

When Ryan and Tatum come in with all the dishes, they're both smiling over whatever conversation they were having in the kitchen.

Tatum looks at me and says, "It's true. I was just telling your sister that one of the troopers was asking about you, Rachel."

I blink. "Asking about *me?*"

Realistically, I know there's only one person who'd be asking about me. But I'm still surprised Michael would bother Tatum about it.

Dad puts his hand on Tatum's arm. "Tate, maybe now isn't the best time for that."

Instead of listening, his girlfriend waves him off and starts setting the table. "Michael Phillips. I bumped into him at the grocery store, and we started talking about our holiday plans. Once he heard you were coming into town, he asked if you were bringing anybody."

It feels like everybody's eyes are on me.

Brie with a frown.

Dad with caution.

Rolling my shoulders over the sound of my high school boyfriend's name, I say, "Dad is right. Now isn't the best time."

Once upon a time, I thought maybe I'd marry him. He told me it was a mistake to break up because we could be a sure thing. And when date after date failed over the last couple of years, I began wondering if he was right. It seemed like I cursed myself by leaving him, and Pennsylvania, behind me.

Tatum pauses, looking at me with an exasperated frown. "Was it really that bad? From what your father told me about the breakup—"

"Why would Dad tell you about my high school relationship ending? That was like seven or eight years ago now. It's insignificant."

Sure, I've seen Michael since. But it was barely anything to write home about. I don't even think I mentioned it to my father unless Brie did.

But that's not what Tatum says. "Your father and I spoke about it when it first happened."

What? I stare at him, slowly trying to connect all the dots from the information I'm being given.

Because Dad said he met Tatum after Mom passed away. But Michael Phillips and I dated my entire four years of high school, breaking up when we were going to different colleges. I'd been confused and sad when I chose to end it and move away, even though I believed it was the better option than having a long-distance relationship.

Dad gives Tatum a warning expression before turning to me. "You were pretty torn up about it at the time, and nothing me or your mother or sister said seemed to help."

If Dad told Tatum about it when it happened, then…

Dad steps toward me, reaching out when he sees the twisted expression on my face as I put two and two together. Because I think my dad cheated on my mom. "It isn't what you think, kiddo."

I jerk my hand away, looking at my sister quizzically. "Did you know about this?"

Tatum intervenes. "Your father was worried about you, Rachel. It was nothing ill-intentioned. He came to me for advice because he thought I might have been where you were before. He wanted an outside perspective."

An outside perspective? Jesus.

"Tatum, enough," Dad tells her in a voice I haven't heard him use on her before. "You're not helping right now."

She straightens at his tone but remains silent when she sees the daggers in my eyes.

Brie clears her throat. "I'm a little fuzzy on the details," she admits, and I'm not sure if she's talking to me or our father. "But I found out a while ago that they knew each other before Mom died. Remember when we messed up my hair during high school by trying to dye it blond and making it orange instead right before picture day? The salon she took me to was where Tatum worked. I guess she kept going back after that."

I take a step back. "Wow."

Dad steps toward me. "Rachel—"

"No, Dad." I hold up my hand, feeling heartbroken for Mom. "There was obviously a reason you lied about when you actually met and started getting to know each other, so don't tell me it was nothing. Mom was *sick*."

Shaking my head, I stare at the man who's lied to me for years. It was bad enough that he moved on from Mom so quickly, but cheating on her when she could barely function? That's a new level of low I didn't think he was capable of.

"I'm not dealing with this," I inform him, walking out of the room.

I don't know where I'm going when I walk into the kitchen and collect my bag and keys. All I know is that I want to get out of here.

Brie walks in after me. "You promised that you'd stay! You can't leave."

"I need air," I tell her. "I need…"

Dad follows me into the kitchen. "If you give me a few minutes to explain—"

"So you can lie again?" I snap. "Pass."

Tatum sighs. "Rachel, you're not being very fair to your father right now."

Is she kidding me? I turn my daggered eyes on her. "And you haven't been fair to any of us since you came into our life, so pot meet kettle."

Brie suddenly blurts out, "I'm pregnant."

Dad and Tatum both turn to her with shocked expressions on their faces.

My sister wiggles her hands like jazz fingers. "Surprise."

Ryan sighs at the announcement. "That's not exactly how we planned on telling you guys."

Still not wanting to be here, I grab my keys. "Congratulations."

Brie's eyes sadden. "Are you coming back? I want time

with you."

I hesitate but eventually nod. "Give me a little time. I'll be back. Okay?"

I look at Dad and shake my head, my stomach sinking. He opens his mouth to try saying something, but I walk out before I hear more bullshit.

When I climb into my car, I pull out my phone and let my thumb hover over the call button next to the new number I saved into my phone when sleep evaded me last night.

Sighing, I put it down before dialing Matt's number and drive off before Dad or Tatum can come out and convince me to come back inside.

WILBER PARK IS pretty this time of year—full of orange, yellow, and red leaves on trees that fall gracefully onto the ground and cover the walking paths for shoes and boots to crunch on. It's shaded, so the park never gets too hot or too cold when you walk the two-mile trail.

Mom used to take Brie and me to the playground here to blow off steam when we were little. When she really wanted to make sure we'd go to bed early, she'd make us walk the trail twice until we were heavy-eyed on the car ride back home.

It's been years since I've been here, and barely anything has changed, save a few tobacco-free signs somebody hung up on the pavilion and the start of the first walking trail.

As the sun starts setting, I regret not changing into something more practical. I hug myself for warmth to fight the cool breeze assaulting my arms in the long-sleeved shirt I'm wearing.

Pulling my phone out, I swipe over all the worried text messages from Brie, Ryan, and Dad that I've ignored over the past few hours of being out and go to my contact list.

I don't bother typing out a message to the number I've never used before. Instead, I hit the call button and listen to it ring. Once. Twice. By the third one, I think I should have held off. It's the holidays. He's probably with his family.

But then he picks up.

Letting out a sharp, relieved breath that he didn't ignore the call, I fight the emotion rising up my throat. "Hi."

There's some shuffling on Matt's end of the phone before a confidant, "Hi, Ruby Red."

Throat bobbing at the familiar nickname, I feel a sense of relief ease my otherwise tense, knotted muscles. "I needed…" My voice cracks, forcing me to clear it. "I needed to talk to someone, and you're the only one I…"

You're the only one I wanted to talk to, is what I can't seem to say. It still feels wrong to gravitate toward the familiarity he offers, but I'd be lying to myself if I said he didn't.

"Are you okay, Rach?"

Sniffling back tears over the events of the day, I shake my head as if he can see me. Swallowing down the lump forming in my throat, I say, "I don't know. I miss my mom. Dumb, right? It's been close to two years, and this empty feeling never goes away whenever I come back here."

Swiping at a few fallen tears, I stare at two bunnies that hop out of the woods and into the pathway. As soon as the bigger one sees me, it nudges the little one back into the tree line.

A mother protecting her baby.

My chest aches.

"I don't think that's dumb at all," Matt reassures me, voices laughing in the background.

Hugging my knees into my chest, I rest my chin on my knees and close my eyes as the breeze pricks at my damp face. "I'm sorry if I'm interrupting your time with family."

"Don't be. Tell me what's going on."

I stare at the trail in front of me, wondering if I should tell him the truth. It takes me a few long seconds before I huff out a quiet sigh. "My mother was still alive when my dad started talking to his new girlfriend, Tatum. It makes me question things. Their love for one another. What the truth is."

Matt is quiet. He knows an apology isn't going to help, so I'm grateful he doesn't give me one.

Sitting up, I use the back of my hand to swipe at my cheeks. "I'm going to be an aunt." I hiccup, smiling as I think about my glowing sister. "Brie is pregnant."

Finally, he says, "That's awesome."

We're silent for a few moments. There's more laughing in the background on his side. Wind on mine. I blow out another short, chilled breath. "I always thought I'd be here when she had kids. When we were younger, we said we'd live next door to one another and raise our kids together."

It's not a faraway thought. Realistically, it could still happen. Someday. But I still don't know if I carry the gene that would make my children motherless if that day ever came. Could I do that to them? Could I risk passing it down and making their own lives hell? Do I even want to know or stay blissfully ignorant like my mother until my very last breath?

Quietly, Matt asks, "Is that what you want?"

I've thought about what comes after graduation. I need my doctorate to become a full-time professor, and the thought of doing a dissertation makes me queasy. But it's not unobtainable. It's also not something I'll be able to do at Lindon. Either way, I'll have to find somewhere else to go. Maybe somewhere in Pennsylvania, closer to Brie, Ryan, and their baby. Or maybe I'll skip my doctorate completely and find a job working for a team somewhere—at a high school or a college. But either way, I know, deep down, I'll regret not being around to watch my niece or nephew grow up.

"Maybe," I admit, not knowing for sure. "But there are drawbacks."

My father, for one.

Tatum, for another.

Could I be around them knowing what I do now? I'm not so sure my sanity could handle it. I feel nauseous even thinking about my father doing anything to ruin what he and my mother had. They were the role models for what a marriage should be, down to the end.

At least, that's what I thought.

"I'm sorry I called," I apologize again, closing my eyes and letting the wind pimple my skin with goose bumps. "It's a holiday, and you're with your family. I shouldn't be bothering you with this when it's not your problem."

He doesn't even hesitate. "My family always says one

thing we're grateful for on the holidays when we're together. It's tradition. I'm grateful that you trusted me enough to call me."

Squeezing my eyelids together to fight off the tears quickly building in the ducts, I let out a pathetic breath that catches in my throat.

Swiping at my eyes with the backs of my hands, I say, "I'm grateful you picked up."

I'm grateful for you.

He doesn't need me to tell him that. He hears it in between the lines.

"If there's anybody who can figure things out, it's you," he tells me genuinely. "But if you want some advice, let your dad explain. Maybe it's not as bad as you think it is."

"And if it is?" I press.

His hesitation doesn't make me feel any better. But his reply does. "Then you'll always have a home in Lindon. With me."

Emotion builds its way back up my throat, forcing me to swallow it down. "And if I decide to move to Pennsylvania?"

I hear a subtle breath exhale from him. "Then maybe I'll find myself in Pennsylvania one day."

It's not the answer I was expecting, making me even more emotional than I was before. Because this boy, this twenty-two, almost twenty-three-year-old, has always been kind to me. Always charming and witty and caring. The soft spot I've had for him since the day we met is uncanny.

Maybe I'll find myself in Pennsylvania one day. Damn. *Damn.* What am I supposed to do with that? If he were here, he'd hear my heart racing in my chest. He'd see the flush to my cheeks that has nothing to do with the cool air.

"Matt…"

"You going to be okay?" he asks, even though there's nothing he could do if I said no. He doesn't dwell on what he said or let me. His nonchalance to the statement echoes in my head though.

Licking my lips, I let it go. "Yes."

"Well, if you need me to send you any more yams for the holiday feast…" he says to lighten the mood.

I crack the tiniest smile. "No yams are needed for this trip. Just…" I pause, biting the inside of my cheek. "Just some clarity."

"I hope you get it, Ruby Red."

The name eases the tightness in my chest a fraction.

He clears his throat. "Happy Thanksgiving, Rach."

After hanging up, I stare at the blank screen before flicking it off. A twig snaps behind me. Then another. Then something warm gets draped over my shoulders, locking them up.

"I thought you might be here," Dad says quietly. "It was her favorite spot too."

Her. Mom.

He sits beside me on the picnic table, staring at the path like he's remembering all the same things I am. My body turns away from him, wanting distance but warmth at the same time.

"I know what you must be thinking," he tells me, eyes roaming over the side of my face despite the way I evade him. "But I never cheated on your mother, Rachel. I loved her very, very much. She was the one who introduced me to

Tatum."

My eyes snap to him. "*What?*"

He nods once, almost sadly. "After Brie's hair fiasco, your mom started going to the salon Tatum worked at more frequently. It was closer and cheaper than her original one, and she liked the hairdressers more. She'd brought up Tatum a few times to me, which I never thought much about. Your mother got along with everybody, so I figured Tate was simply another friend she'd made. When your mother's disease started progressing, I had to start taking her places when she couldn't get around as easily on her own. She never wanted to give up her salon days because it was a chance for her to feel pampered, so I'd drive her. I wanted her to have those moments, no matter what."

I remember how upset Mom was that she couldn't drive herself places, but Dad never thought twice about taking her wherever she needed to go. He was happy to bring her to get her hair or her nails done because he knew she needed that. It made her feel pretty during her battle with the ugly disease.

"I didn't know Tate very well at first," he continues to explain. "Not until much later. Our conversations were nothing more than small talk for a long time. Your mother and she did most of the talking whenever we went to the salon."

I shake my head and look at him with narrowed eyes. "That obviously changed. I doubt Mom willingly introduced you to her replacement."

Dad winces. "I don't like that word."

Something tells me he wouldn't approve of the other

words I've used in my head whenever I think of Tatum or their relationship.

He sighs when he sees I'm not interested in changing it. "Oh, my ray of sunshine. You're so much like your mother; it sometimes kills me a little."

I frown, huddling into the jacket he put around me.

Dad puts his arm around my shoulder. "It always scared me how fierce you were because of her. She raised two strong-headed girls that are forces to be reckoned with."

My eyes go to my lap, where I'm squeezing my hands together tightly. Unsure of what to say, I remain silent.

He doesn't need me to say anything. "It makes sense why you'd jump to the conclusion that you did about Tate and me. I'm not asking you to think of her as a mother—" I scoff at the notion, making him sigh. "I'm not even asking you to like her. But I don't want you thinking she got in between your mother and me when that was the furthest thing from the truth. Toward the end, your mother…"

His long-winded pause has me finally glancing in his direction with curiosity. "Toward the end, your mother encouraged me to move on. To live my life and show you and your sister that it's okay to be happy even after she's gone. It wasn't something I wanted to hear at the time, but she knew it was what I *needed* to."

It's the last thing I want to hear too. How could Mom tell him to find somebody else? She was dying. That's the last thing she should have been focusing on.

"There will never be another woman like your mother," Dad whispers, tugging me into his side and rubbing my arm. "Because if I were in her shoes, I wouldn't want to think about the life my family is living after I'm gone. Even if I hope they're loved and happy without me."

Tears burn the backs of my eyes. Mom sacrificed so much of her life for us until her very last breath. The one thing she said she always wanted to be when she was older was a mother—to have a family she was devoted to, no matter the circumstances.

She wanted Dad to fall in love again and Brie and me to know it was okay to mourn but also okay to move on. To be happy. Even without her in our lives to share it with.

Letting out a shaky breath, I take a deep breath and count to three before exhaling. "You didn't have to fall in love so quickly," I whisper, still hurt by the betrayal that's sunk its claws into me since he said he was seeing somebody.

His hold on me tightens. "I know, baby girl. I know."

It's not an apology.

It's an olive branch.

"One day," he tells me, "You'll understand that love can make you do things you never thought you would. That's all your mother and I could ever hope for you and your sister."

My mind goes back to Matt, who is the last person I should be thinking about.

Swallowing, I look at him. "Yeah. Maybe you're right."

He rubs my back. "Ready to go home?"

Home. I hug my legs into my chest and rest my cheek on my bent knees. "You're going to be a grandfather."

He smiles. "I am."

I look away, raw emotion overheating my face and neck. "Mom would have been so excited," I say, sad she can't be here to witness Brie as a mother.

His hand pauses before squeezing my shoulder. "She would have."

We sit in silence.

"I miss her too," he admits.

I look at him.

He's not looking at me though. "Every day."

I watch him—the same emotion on my face shadowing his features as his eyes get glassy.

He really does miss her.

"I miss everything about back then," he adds, not giving me the specifics. He doesn't need to.

He misses her. And me. And Brie. He misses the good days. The bad days. He misses when we were a *family*.

Sometimes, I miss that too.

I stand, accepting the invisible olive branch by reaching out to him and squeezing his hand once. "Let's go home."

There were candied yams and no raisins in the stuffing or dairy in the mac and cheese this Thanksgiving.

It wasn't perfect.

But it was…better.

CHAPTER FIFTEEN

Matt

THE REST OF the semester goes by quickly, and a large part of that has to do with how busy classes have kept me. As finals approach, I spend a lot of time in Rachel's office going over study materials for the two classes I struggled the most in. Each night, I bring something for us to eat, and we spend the first thirty minutes talking about life. The upcoming holidays. Winter break. How the semester went. She tells me she made up with her father and was going to spend time with them over winter break. I tell her my parents are going on a cruise after Christmas, and I'll be spending most of the break alone. I don't ask her to come by, even if the temptation to is on the tip of my tongue.

I don't pry about what she's going to do next semester when she finishes grad school. Mostly because I don't want to know if she's made up her mind. If she has, and it's not staying here, I'll have half a year to wonder what I could do to make her stay and, inevitably, watch her go, knowing it's not my place to. I meant what I said.

She has a home here. A family here.

Lindon has been my home my whole life, but I know it isn't hers. And I understand why she'd want to go. Her sister is there. Her father. I can't change that.

Eventually, finals finish, and Christmas break is days away. I passed each one of my exams and my classes with flying colors, just like she said I would. Which is why I show up to Rachel's office during our normal meeting time wearing a cheap Santa suit that I bought online and throw a pillowcase as a toy sack over my shoulder.

When she sees me, she laughs.

And the soft sound reminds me why this office is one of my favorite places in the world.

"Christmas is still a few days away," she reminds me with an amused shake of her head as I dig through my pillowcase and pull out a box with her name on it.

It took me two hours and a lot of YouTube videos to figure out how to wrap this thing without using a whole roll of tape. I'd nearly given up when I tried getting the ribbon to look decent, but I'm happy with the results. Mostly because I didn't have to ask my mother for help for once.

"You didn't have to get me anything," she says, her smile small but warm as I pass it to her.

I smile. "I know, but I wanted to. You've been helping me a lot lately, so I wanted to thank you. And don't try fighting it and telling me it's inappropriate to accept. Just take it."

"I was happy to help," she says, nibbling her lip and shaking it gently to try figuring out what's inside. "Plus, you bought us food every time you came here. That adds up."

The confusion pinching her face as she stares at the packaging makes me chuckle as she undoes the ribbon and tears the paper.

I sit down and hold my breath when she lifts the lid and

stares inside.

A little breath escapes her as she pulls out the first edition copy of *The Wonderful Wizard of Oz*. It took me months of searching for the book before finally finding it online, and I was grateful it didn't completely break the bank.

"Matt," she whispers in awe, her fingers grazing the worn cover. Her eyes lift. "This is…"

I wave her speechlessness off, feeling my cheeks heat. I was afraid she wouldn't like it, but those hazel eyes tell me everything I need to know.

"It isn't a big deal."

All she does is stare, her throat bobbing with a swallow. Her parted lips and soft gaze tell me it is to her.

Rubbing the back of my neck, I say, "I really appreciate everything you've done for me this semester. Not having football and getting used to a new routine wasn't easy for me. You made things easier. I wanted to find a way to thank you for that."

She silently shakes her head, her gaze dipping back down to the book in her hands. After what feels like forever, she says, "You never have to thank me. I was more than happy to help, Matt. Truthfully, I missed the familiarity I had last year. You brought me that."

The words ring in my head, inflating my chest with a swell of pride. "You're admitting you like me."

She rolls her eyes, her lips kicking up in the corners. "Don't let it get to your head."

I chuckle. "Too late."

She bites down on her bottom lip. "I know you miss football and the way things used to be. Have you thought about next year? If you're coming back to finish school."

The last thing I want to feel like is a failure. I've always prided myself on finishing what I started. But grad school...it's not for everyone. I've learned that. And do I really need a master's degree in finance? No. The problem is, the one thing that bores me more than school is the thought of working in a bank the rest of my life.

Truthfully, I'm lost. "I don't know yet."

I'm greeted with a sympathetic smile. "Well, you have some time."

"It'd be easier if someone chose for me," I mumble, wishing that were an option.

Rachel sets the book down. "That's not how life works, unfortunately."

We're quiet for a long time, simply watching one another. It's not an awkward silence or a tense one. She smiles. I smile back.

"For what it's worth," she finally says. "I'm proud of you. And I really do believe that you'll find something that makes you happy. You just need to keep working for it."

Find something that makes you happy.

If she only knew.

Scratch that.

If she only *accepted* what we both know.

Because she makes me happy. Football makes me happy. Being part of something like a team makes me happy.

The longer we stare at each other, the thicker the atmosphere gets around us. Can she hear my thoughts? Does she see the way I look at her? My heart does some weird backflip in its cage when I see her top front teeth dig into her full bottom lip like she knows exactly what's on my mind.

I walk around the desk, stopping just shy of her. She looks up, worry and something else in the hues. I'd like to think it's love or something close, but I don't let myself think about it for too long.

I bend down and hug her because I don't want to risk losing what we've managed to build after the last time.

In my mind, I say, *I think I love you.* At least, it feels like that's what's happening. Every time she's near, my heart jerks. She's always on my mind. Her encouragement drives me. Her words of affirmation motivate me. Rachel has become a big part of my life here in Lindon.

But I don't say any of that out loud. "I know I will," I tell her instead. "I know we both will. Someday."

More staring.

A small breath escapes her.

"Merry Christmas, Ruby Red."

Her throat bobs. "Merry Christmas, Matt."

Pulling away, I look at her lips. They part as she sucks in a slow, deep breath. I can feel her warm breath, and it makes my heart drum harder in its cage when I feel it reflect off my face.

"Do you have any more meetings today?" I ask, eyes still studying the slight curve of her bottom lip as she pulls it farther into her mouth. I suddenly remember all the times I nibbled it during our drunken tryst over a year ago that caused subtle noises to rise from her throat.

"No." Her answer is no more than a whisper.

Eyes lifting from her mouth to her eyes, I see the darkened orbs I can only assume are from the same lust building inside me. "Good."

I close the space between us, dipping my head down until my mouth is over hers and swallowing the gasp she releases.

The kiss is heated and rushed—a mixture of soft-spoken sighs and heady groans.

I missed this. Missed *her*.

Using my foot to connect with the door, I close it. I find the lock and flick it until we're safely secured inside, barely breaking contact.

Lifting her up, I set her on the edge of the desk and knead her fleshy hips with my fingers until my dick hardens in my jeans and stupid Santa suit.

This isn't what I came in here for, but I'll be damned if I want to stop now. But when my hips arch forward of their own accord to chase the friction I desperately need, I all but groan when my dick rubs against her thigh.

It takes everything in me to pull even an inch away, breathing heavy. Leaning my forehead against hers, I close my eyes and try focusing on anything but the relief I'm aching for. "Stop going on dates," I tell her. "Please."

Her body stiffens for a fraction before she leans back to look me in the eye. Her lips are puffy from my kisses, and it gives me an odd sense of satisfaction. "Matt…"

"If they were important enough, if they *mattered*, this wouldn't be happening," I point out, fingertips digging into her hips. "You would have kept seeing at least one of them. But you never did."

She can't argue with me because she knows it's the truth. And it isn't because I came in and ruined them. She had plenty of opportunities to salvage those nights, but she chose not to.

Rachel never chose any of those men. She always chose *me*, whether she knew it or not.

"If you liked any of them," I say, lips trailing up her jaw. "If you thought there was even a *possibility* that they could make you feel the way I am—" I murmur, trailing a hot path of kisses to her ear. "—then I wouldn't be between your legs right now."

I nip the bottom of her lobe, making her shiver. Grinning against her when I hear the subtle exhale she releases, I brush my lips over her cheek.

Once.

Twice.

I stop at the corner of her mouth.

Waiting.

Waiting for her to tell me to stop.

Waiting for her to tell me I'm wrong.

She does neither.

"Tell me I'm wrong," I challenge, my lips ghosting over hers in a barely there touch.

Rachel's lips part just enough to brush mine, her breath teasing my mouth. "I can't."

My grin stretches, but it doesn't last long before I'm kissing her again. It's hot and heavy and addicting. Hands trailing down the curve of her backside, I squeeze once before pulling her toward me until she can feel how hard I am.

Swallowing her soft moan with my mouth to drown out the noise, I let my hand move down her thigh until it reaches the hem of her skirt. "I suggest you be very, very quiet if you don't want people to know what's happening in here," I tell her as my fingers dance along the inside of her thigh until they reach the apex where her cotton panties greet my fingertips.

Face flushed, she bites down on her bottom lip when I coast my knuckles along the sensitive skin between her thighs.

"I love how responsive you are," I say, peppering kisses down her throat as I work her with my hand. How many times have I thought about our first time together, praying for a repeat? I touched myself almost every night for two weeks following that, thinking about the memories of every little thing I did to her.

There's a sting of pain from where her fingers dig into my shoulders, but I live for it, knowing it's because I'm making her feel good.

I know when she's close to release because her legs squeeze my arm as she starts squirming where she's hanging from the edge of the desk.

"That's it," I praise, my head dipping to the crook of her neck to nip and lick and suck the spot above her pulse. "Let go, Rach. I've got you."

Her grip tightens as her thighs clench me until her mouth falls open in a silent orgasm.

I watch her, transfixed by the way her eyelashes flutter and her head tilts back and she absorbs the moment as I work her through her release until she's sated.

When she looks at me, her chest rising and falling rapidly, all she says is, "Please."

And that breathless plea is all I need. I grab her and turn her around, bending her over the desk and lifting her skirt to reveal her perky, round ass in a pair of white panties that make her look so pure.

So innocent.

But we both know she's not.

After hastily tugging down the costume pants and undoing my jeans to pull myself out, I slip on a condom and trace the edges of her panties with my finger. "Remember to be a good girl and keep quiet," I whisper, before pulling her underwear aside, gently parting her legs to give myself more room between them and lining myself up.

I know it's not going to be a long experience because it's been a while, and I know the second I slide between these pretty thighs of hers, it's going to be like the first goddamn time. Dangerous. Tight. Warm.

So, I give her all I have, surging forward and covering her mouth with my palm when she makes a noise that could easily get us found out.

She bites down on my finger as I work both of us up with every jackknife of my hips. I have to swallow every appreciative groan that rises to the surface when I hear her body react to me being inside of her, doing my best to take the brunt of the impact so her hips aren't slamming against the wooden desk too hard.

Using my free hand, I bend her knee up to rest on the edge of the desk to give myself a deeper angle and—

"*Jesus Christ,*" I rasp, feeling her clench around me.

The desk starts moving slowly, the legs scraping against the bottom of the floor and making a hideous noise against the linoleum. I don't know why, but it makes me lose control.

My hand, holding her leg up, slides between her legs to rub the nerves that have her moaning around my finger as I pick up the pace and feel the telltale tingle shooting down my spine before I thrust forward one more time and empty myself into the condom.

We stay like that, my hands pulling away to rub her back, her shoulders, and her side as I gently pull out and dispose of the condom.

She looks over her shoulder at me, her face pink and her lips swollen. I can't help but grin, knowing I did that to her.

But those glassy eyes that I love having pointed in my direction seem to hold something else that slightly dims the color.

"Rach?" I ask quietly, caressing her arm.

She swallows, flattening out the wrinkles in her outfit after redressing and combing her fingers through her hair. "You're right," she says softly, not looking me in the eye. "If any of those guys mattered, you wouldn't be here." I don't have time to celebrate the admission when she adds, "But that doesn't make this right."

I stare at her silently.

She's not looking at me.

She's looking at the present I gave her.

I see her throat bob, contemplation like a wave over her features that wipes out the lust and satisfaction we both felt moments earlier.

"I don't regret it," I tell her honestly.

How could I? She's the only person I find myself constantly gravitating to. When I'm sad. When I'm happy. When I'm angry. It's her who makes it better, no matter the circumstances.

I've never been in love before, not really. But I'm pretty sure this is the closest I've come. Because love isn't just a feeling—it's a decision. A judgment. Right or wrong, I'll keep choosing the girl in front of me.

Instead of pushing her to talk to me, to tell me she doesn't regret it either, I simply say, "Have a good break, Rach."

That night, I get a text message from the woman I walked away from nearly five hours before.

Ruby Red: *I don't regret it either*

CHAPTER SIXTEEN

Rachel

B RIE DEVOURS ALMOST the entire large bowl of popcorn sitting between us as we watch *The Wizard of Oz* for the millionth time. But it never gets old. None of this does. Not the comfy matching holiday pajamas, or the thick blankets draped over us, or the lights dimmed while a movie we love plays. I've missed this. Watching TV in my apartment doesn't feel the same. There's no sarcastic commentary from my sister or anybody to share my snacks with.

"So what next?" Brie asks as the screen fades away when the film ends.

I stretch and yawn when I see that it's already past midnight. "I don't know. Bed?"

She frowns. "You're no fun."

"How are you even awake?" I ask. I know for a fact Ryan said she napped now more than she ever has before. "I thought pregnancy made women extra tired or something."

"I took a nap before you got here."

Of course she did.

"We've already watched all the Christmas classics," I tell her, staring at the pile of DVDs on the table that we've been through. "And your husband passed out hours ago. I'm sure he's wondering where you are."

Brie waves me off, moving the empty bowl away from us and setting it on the table. "He'll be fine. I want time with my big sis. Are you excited to be in your last semester of school?"

I'm not sure excited is the right word. Nervous. Anxious. A little sad. All of those are much more fitting. "It's nerve-racking," I admit.

I've never been great with the unknown. My adviser gave me some information on a few PhD programs for my doctorate degree, but I'm still not sold on the next steps, or where those steps will take me.

Brie shifts on the couch, her hand absentmindedly going to her midsection and palming the tiny bump there. Unless you were clued in, you'd never know she was pregnant by just looking at her. "I don't know how you managed to suffer through so much schooling. I barely passed high school. The thought of going to college…" Her face scrunches. "I've always respected you a lot for everything you've done."

I blink, a little surprised by her admission. It's not that I've ever felt she hasn't respected me for my choices in life, but I've let myself live with the guilt of leaving her behind to pursue those decisions. "Really?"

She rolls her eyes, grinning at me. "Yes, really, dummy. You've always been so sure of everything you've wanted, and you work so hard for it all. I wish I had half as much motivation as you do." Her smile slowly disappears, not turning into a frown, but making her look thoughtful. "I used to be jealous of you."

My eyebrows shoot up my forehead.

She nods, lifting her shoulders. "You're so much like Mom, and you followed in her footsteps. I've always sort of felt like a failure because I never wanted to go to college or be a teacher. I used to think she wouldn't be proud of me because I took a different route."

My heart drops into my stomach. How could she think that? "Brie Cheese, Mom could never be disappointed in you. She always used to tell us she was happy if we were, remember? Like when we both were at the dating age. She told us she didn't care if the person we brought home was white, black, or purple as long as they treated us right and made us happy. Or when we became seniors, and she said she was okay with whatever we chose to do after high school as long as we made a future for ourselves. There was nobody more supportive than her. *You* get that from her."

I can tell my little sister doesn't believe me, but it's true. Even when she was sad I was leaving, she told me she was happy for me. And even though she'd been upset that I wasn't moving back to Pennsylvania immediately after our mother died, she understood I needed space from here. I'm not sure I would have felt the same if I were in her shoes.

That's our mother through and through.

I grab her hand and hold it. "I have no doubt in my mind that Mom is so, so proud of you. She's proud of both of us. And there are things…" I wince, thinking about all the stuff I'd rather she'd not see me do. "There are things I'm sure she wouldn't approve of us doing sometimes, but that doesn't change how she loves us. Even from wherever she's watching us from. You're working a good job with good benefits and a good paycheck. You're married to the love of your life and bringing the very first grandbaby into the world. Just because you didn't follow in her footsteps doesn't mean she would love you any less for it."

Her eyes go down to her stomach, which her other hand is still palming. A soft smile splits her mouth, making her ease her squared shoulders.

Then her eyes bolt up to mine, her brows pinched. "Wait a minute. What kinds of things would she not approve of that you're doing? You're, like, the golden child."

I snort before I can stop myself. "I've never been called that before."

"Well, you are. So tell me what you did."

"Nothing…"

She sits up straighter. "Oh my God. It has to do with a boy."

I gape at her. "How do you—"

The high-pitched squeal of excitement hurts my ears as she claps. "I'm right! This is so exciting. Your dating life is so boring, it's about time you spilled the tea."

"Hey." I frown. "It's not that boring."

"The last guy you told me about was some IT nerd who lived in his parents' basement."

I wince. "He was saving money to buy his first house. It's not that uncommon for people to live with their parents these days. Have you kept up with the economy?"

She eyes me, ignoring the question for one of her own. "What about the guy who sold cars for a living and thought he was going to be some Google tech wizard in Cali?"

Ugh. Dylan. I wish I could forget that date. Secretly, I was a little glad that Matthew salvaged the night. "I get it. I don't have great judgment. But these guys seemed decent over messaging. It just didn't convert to in-person conversations."

Brie scoffs. "That's because the IT dork was probably only used to talking to middle-aged men about side quests and *Star Wars* over gaming headphones. I'm sure you were the first woman he ever spoke to."

"That's a little mean," I chide. But also, possibly not untrue. Which is sad.

"And the car salesman probably doesn't even know what a clit is, much less where to find it," she states confidently.

I can't help but snort at that.

"I bet he thinks it's a fictional thing women made up," she muses with a snicker. "And the only time he tried finding it turned into him strumming the lips like a guitar and asking the poor girl if she came yet."

Now, I'm belly laughing so hard my stomach hurts, and I have to smack my sister for her crudeness. "Don't be gross," I say in between gasps of breath.

She shrugs it off. "So, tell me. Who's the guy, and why would Mom not approve? Is he super old and wrinkly? Like grandad's age?"

What the hell? "Gross. No." I don't even want to know why her mind would go there.

"Okay. So…" Her eyes narrow in contemplation as she stares at me, the tip of her tongue dipping out the corner of her mouth as she racks her brain for another reason. Then her expression melts into one of shock. "He's married. You're into a married guy. God, Rach! Did you *sleep with him*? What about his wife and kids?"

Holy shit. Not only is she assuming the worst, but she's making me a home-wrecker to a fictional family. "Brie," I say slowly, blinking. "There's no married man. Or children."

For a moment, it looks like she doesn't believe me. Then she blows out a long breath and nods. "Okay. Good. Even *I* would judge you for that. Especially since you got your panties in a twist over the Dad and Tatum thing."

My eye twitches. Even though that was cleared up during Thanksgiving break, it still hits me in the chest like a sledgehammer to the heart. I'm trying to put it behind me—to be happy for Dad the way Mom wanted him to be. But all those feelings, grief, mourning, and confusion don't just go away overnight. I wish it did. For my sake. For Dad's. Even maybe for Tatum's. A little.

But the thing is, I'm still a hypocrite. I may not be a cheater or a home-wrecker, but I did cross ethical boundaries with somebody younger than me. Isn't that something I've judged my father for since he told us about Tatum? She's only ten years older than me. Not even a full ten years. More like nine and a half. And, sure, I wasn't going after anybody underage. But it doesn't look good considering my feelings about my father's current relationship.

Brie squeezes my hand. "What is it then?"

Would she judge me? Tell me I'm gross? That I'm wrong for what I've done or how I feel? Because what I feel...

Well, it's too much. I feel alive with Matt. Like I'm a teenager again. We may not be that different in age, but he makes me feel younger, carefree, and...happy.

Just like Mom always wanted me to be.

Internally, I sigh. "There's this boy..."

She makes another squealing sound that makes me flinch.

"Stop doing that before you wake up Ryan," I grumble, rubbing my ear. Counting to three, I decide to rip off the Band-Aid and tell her. "There is a boy named Matt who used to play for the Dragons. We sort of…" Does she really need me to go into details? "Well, we may have slept together once. Or twice—"

"You ho!" she says with a huge grin on her face, shoving my shoulder. "All this time, I thought your vagina has cobwebs. I didn't know you hired a football-playing housekeeper to take care of all that dust."

Seriously? "Brie, it's not a good thing."

"Is he at least eighteen?"

"Yes."

"So he's legal," she says with a shrug. "Is he hot? Oh, no. He's ugly, isn't he? Did he take too many hits to the face or something? Because I thought that was only a wrestling thing. They make football players wear helmets for a reason."

I have to close my eyes and pinch the bridge of my nose. This conversation isn't going how I expected. Then again, it's not a bad thing. She's not calling me a disgusting human or a hypocrite.

I'll take that as a win.

When I finally open my eyes, I feel calmer. "I really shouldn't expect any less from you, but I'm still reeling at how this is going."

Brie is unashamed. "Look, it's okay if he's ugly. Beauty is subjective."

I groan. "He isn't ugly."

"Okay…"

"He's a few years younger than me."

She blinks silently.

"And a student," I say, a little quieter.

Understanding takes a few minutes to cross her face before she lets out a drawn-out, "Ohhhh. I see." But I don't think she really does. "Is that against the rules or something?"

My eyebrow twitches. "Yes."

"But you're a student too."

"But I'm also a faculty member," I point out.

I read the rulebook. Twice. And after Coach Pearce's abrupt exit, it was abundantly clear that nobody else make any mistakes that would cost more scandal in the news. The university already lost funding thanks to the articles published about the former head coach's broken moral compass. They don't want any repeats, no matter the circumstances.

Now Brie actually gets it. "And you think Mom wouldn't approve because you're going against the rules," she states.

All I do is nod.

"That's stupid," she informs me. "You just said that Mom would be happy for us, no matter what. Does Matt make you happy?"

"Well…"

Her brows arch. "Well, what?"

Quietly, I say, "Yes."

"And he's older than eighteen, so he's legal," she adds, using another finger on her hand to point out that I'm being ridiculous. "Plus, you said he's a former player on the team, which means you probably don't work with him anymore. It isn't like he's in a class you teach. He's not young and naive. I'm sure he knows what he's getting himself into."

Does he though? It hasn't seemed like he understood the ramifications of getting caught. How different they would be for me than for him. I still have a lot to risk.

Yet, you risked it anyway.

God, I really am a ho.

"It isn't like you banged him on your desk at work or anything," she says nonchalantly.

I make a face before I can stop myself, causing my sister to gasp.

"Holy damn, you slut. You totally banged him on your desk at work. I'm..." She looks like she's getting emotional. "I'm so proud of you."

Oh my God. "Brie," I grumble, sighing. Is that a tear? Jesus. She's literally crying. "Are you really getting all weepy on me?"

She sniffles. "It's these stupid pregnancy hormones. Shut up." Swiping under her eyes, she takes a deep breath. "Look, I don't see what the big deal is. You're graduating soon. If you want to be with him, if you love him, it isn't like you have to wait for long."

"Whoa," I stop her, eyes widening. "I never said I loved him."

She rolls her glassy eyes. "Rachel, you're so dense some-times. Don't do the same thing you did with Michael."

What? "What are you talking about?"

"Why didn't things work out with Michael?" she asks.

Ugh, random. "We wanted different things. He wanted to be a cop here, and I wanted to leave. You know that."

She shakes her head. "That's not it, though. You broke up with him because you got in your head. Even you admitted that he never said that you couldn't go away to college or have a career of your own. You told yourself that so you could justify going."

"I…" I stop myself, lips parting.

Then I think about it. Really think.

Brie's expression softens. "Michael has always been stubborn, but he also loved you a lot. I'm sure he would have been willing to do long-distance if you truly wanted to get away. And even if his dream was to be a cop here, he could have found a job in law enforcement anywhere. I'm sure he would have for you."

For once, I'm speechless.

Because…she's right. Michael probably would have done all those things. He was a good person. A really good one.

Brie takes my hand again. "You're always overthinking everything. Maybe it's time you got out of that thick skull of yours and let your heart decide what to do for once. If this guy didn't matter, you wouldn't be worried if Mom would approve or not. He matters to you because you love him."

My whole body warms up at the proclamation that I've never truly said. But…

I think she's right.

Nibbling on my lip, I release it and lean back on the couch. "I've given Dad and Tatum a lot of shit for their relationship."

My sister smiles warmly. "It's not too late to apologize

for that."

I look down at my lap.

We sit in silence for what feels like forever.

Then Brie breaks it by saying, "Did you really have sex on your desk?" My face heats up, making her even more interested in the answer. "I need the details. And maybe some ice cream."

✪

THE FRONT STOOP of my childhood home is cold as I stare up absentmindedly at the New Year's fireworks display happening in the distance. A harsh wind snatches the knit cap off my head before I can catch it, blowing it away, and I welcome the brutal chill.

Before I can even bother getting up to catch it, I see it extended to me by a petite hand with manicured fingers that can only belong to one person. "Mind if I join you?" Tatum asks, waiting for me to shake my head before sitting on the cool cement beside me. "It's a little cold to be out here. You'll get sick."

"I needed fresh air."

She stuffs her hands into her winter jacket and watches the pretty colors explode across the dark sky. "I know I'm the last person you probably want to talk to, but your dad is worried. You've been quiet, and you haven't eaten much since coming home. Are you feeling okay?"

Mom's appetite dulled when her disease progressed. She didn't talk because she struggled to. Her mind was cloudy, and her energy was low. If he's worried, I'm sure it's because of that.

"I didn't mean to worry him," I tell her, hugging my arms around my torso. Despite the thick down jacket, the chilly air still seeps in. "I have a lot on my mind, that's all."

That's a partial lie.

Sure, going back to Lindon and thinking about what I'll say to Matt is giving me heartburn. I still don't know what I'm going to do. My adviser told me I needed to give her a decision on where to get my doctorate in the next month to start the application process. There is a lot of uncertainty riding on my choices over the next few weeks.

Maybe if that was all that was resting on my shoulders, I could manage it better. But then I walked into my childhood home on Christmas Day and saw it. The Christmas tree. Not with the white lights that were normally strung along the seven-foot tree, but colorful ones that flashed. Mom hated those. She also didn't like the white fluffy tree skirts because they reminded her of snow. She hated snow.

And then there were the stockings...

Or, more specifically, the lack of certain stockings hanging on the wall.

Mom's stocking was missing. Erased just like her favorite yellow walls, white curtains, and area rug, which she had imported all the way from Italy because she loved it so much when she and Dad went on their honeymoon.

When I saw that, I think my heart actually cracked.

I couldn't talk.

Couldn't eat.

Mom's favorite holiday was Christmas, and there was no memory of her in sight this year.

Tatum's eyes study my profile, a long breath releasing into a puff of air in front of her when she faces forward again. "I know you and I will never be friends, but we have things in common. We both love your father."

My nostrils flare with irritation, and I stay quiet. I don't trust myself to comment on that because it'll be driven by emotions.

Then Tatum says something I wasn't anticipating. "My aunt died in a car accident when I was twenty-one. It was...horrific. A drunk driver struck her car, killing her and one of their passengers."

Sadness sweeps over me. "That's horrible," I whisper, frowning when I see the distant look she has on her face. "I'm sorry to hear that."

She nods almost absently before looking at me with a tiny smile. "I appreciate that. I'm only telling you because I saw what it did to my uncle. He was so lost. So depressed. They were the perfect couple everybody looked up to. Even I was a little jealous of them." Her expression is thoughtful, nostalgic. "Losing her was like losing an organ. I've never seen him that way in my life. I watched him disappear a little more every day until there was barely anything left."

Sounds familiar. For the first couple of months, Dad was inconsolable. Brie and I tried everything we could to get him to eat. He barely went to work. Slept a lot. I thought he was going to lose his job at the bank because of all the time he took off. They were understanding...at first. Then, they were less so as time went on. Not that I blamed them.

"It took a long time for him to be okay," she continues softly. "And a lot of therapy. I went to a few sessions with him because my aunt meant the absolute world to me too. She practically raised me because of how much my parents worked. She was my best friend. Talking about it helped, and coming up with solutions for moving forward was something my uncle and I had to work toward. But we did. Eventually.

"It started with little things but led to much larger changes. We redid his bedding. Then, the living room pillows. After a while, we repainted the house. She was the one who decorated everything. Chose the colors and the décor. Revamping things was cheaper than buying a new house…"

I see where she's going with this, but I don't know how I feel about it. "My father isn't your uncle," I tell her. "And my mom isn't your aunt. Your uncle and my father lost somebody special to them. Repainting a house and buying new pillows isn't going to change that. Their memories don't deserve to be erased just because they're gone."

She leans back, looking up at the fireworks still lighting the sky in red, white, and blue formations. "I promise I'm not trying to make your father forget anything. All her things are in a custom-made box I got for him shortly after she passed. It's the same type of box I got my uncle for his late wife. You're supposed to put things that remind you of them inside. It doesn't have to be every day or every week. It's on your timeline. A memory box, they call it. Your mother will always be with you and your father and sister, Rachel. Always."

I want to blame her. Be angry. Call her names.

But she *has* made a difference in Dad's life, even if I hate the changes she's made to the house. Truthfully, I think she could be right. Maybe. Change isn't always bad. And the way Dad was right after Mom's passing…

"I know that there's no replacing the woman your mom was. Not her memory or her character or her role. And I don't want to, Rachel. That was never my intention when I fell for your dad. Neither was accepting that the future I always wanted and the future I've gotten are two different things."

"What do you mean?" This is the most we've spoken to each other in all the time I've known her, so I don't expect her to give me an honest answer. But she does.

"I always wanted to get married and have kids of my own," she admits, staring up at the sky. "But your father doesn't want to repeat either of those things, and I've learned to be okay with it. Because I love him, and he loves you and Brie. What we have is enough."

All I can do is stare at her in disbelief.

She's willing to stay with my father despite not getting what she wants from their relationship?

"I don't expect us to be friends," she reiterates, dropping her feet onto the ground and knocking our shoulders together. "But I wouldn't mind a shot to be…whatever it is you might need right now. For whatever that's worth."

She isn't pushing or pressing or being unreasonable. Has she always been like this? I feel a little bad I haven't tried harder to get to know her like Dad has wanted.

"If I tell you something, can you not bring it up to Dad until I'm ready to tell him?" My eyes peek at her with vulnerability, rubbing my arm for warmth.

"I can manage that."

Swallowing, I look around the decorated front yard with a blow-up reindeer and Santa sleigh and candy cane lights lining the walkway to the house. I count to three and say, "I think I want to come home. For Brie and the baby. And for Dad."

For a moment, surprise flickers on her face. Then a slow, warm smile splits her lips.

Moving my hair out of my face, I cluck my tongue thoughtfully. "It's only a thought."

Her hand touches mine lightly to gain my attention, only briefly, before pulling away. "If that's what you truly want to do, I know everybody will happily support you. Me included. Your father has been hoping you'd come back, but he knows you need to live your life the way you want to. He'd never influence you one way or another."

I nod thoughtfully, staying quiet.

"I won't say a word," she promises, standing up and brushing herself off. "But you should come in before you catch something. I think I heard your father say he was going to make some hot chocolate."

My eyes lift. "With the mini marshmallows?"

Her smile stretches as she extends a hand out to me. "He bought a new bag when you said you'd be spending the entire break with us."

I stare at her hand for a moment longer.

Then I take it.

CHAPTER SEVENTEEN

Matt

THE TWO COFFEES in my hands warm my palms from the cold air nipping at my skin. Stepping into Anders Hardware is an instant relief when the heat encompasses my otherwise frosted body. The cold snap that hit the northern east coast made it abnormally cold. It took everything in me to come here when Caleb told me to meet him to talk about something.

"Hey," I greet, passing the former running back one of the cups I got from Bea's Bakery. "It looks great in here. You've done a lot of work."

Ever since his dad passed away before the new year, he's been working ten times harder on cleaning up the store and trying to drum up business again. DJ and I have helped him a few times, but I think he prefers the quiet time to himself because it makes him feel closer to his father.

"What did you want to talk to me about?" I ask, leaning against the countertop. "You said something about whatever it is being a good opportunity for me."

Normally, he isn't so vague. But my curiosity was piqued enough to drag my ass out of bed and bear the cold.

"You know a kid on the football team named Wells? He's one of the new running backs that took over my position."

I rack my brain for a face to go with the name. It sounds familiar, but I can't picture anybody off the top of my head. "I don't know. Maybe? I've only been to a few of the games. One of the new coaches is a fucking snake, so I don't really feel like going and watching him fuck up the team more than Pearce did toward the end."

Okay, maybe it's judgmental of me to call *Coach Kelly* a snake since I'm mostly bitter about his obvious interest in Rachel. But still. He hasn't exactly built a name for himself at Lindon. Certainly not like Pearce did.

"I'm actually kind of glad you said that," Caleb says.

Confusion twists my expression.

He shuffles through his bag until he produces a piece of paper, sliding it across the counter toward me.

"You thought of me when you saw a job posting for the university?" I ask in confusion.

"It's for coaching. Wells came up to me a while ago saying he thought I should consider it, but I had way too much on my plate to even entertain the idea. Then I wondered if I should reach out to someone in HR because they're willing to pay for grad school during my employment."

I look up at him from the paper. "Why didn't you reach out then? If they could take some of that stress off your shoulders, then it's worth a conversation."

He's been stressed about grad school—paying for it and having the time to go to classes and take over the store. They don't have much help here, especially not when he's at school.

"I'm actually going to be taking a break after this semester. Right now, I want my attention to go to the store and family stuff. Dad was right. I don't need this degree. If I change my mind, I'll come back to it, but I have other things to focus on. Adding coaching into my schedule would have been impossible when I barely had time to even get my schoolwork done as it is now. It's not in the cards for me."

I frown at the thought of losing my friend. I'd still have DJ, but still. Damn. "That sucks, man. So you're leaving the university in May?"

"Don't miss me yet. I'll obviously be here, and you know where my apartment is. But yeah. It's time for me to step back and stop trying to do it all, like you guys keep telling me."

I've been trying to tell him that all semester, whenever we'd find time to meet up. He's been beating himself up for not being able to juggle a million things at once. The poor guy thinks he can be Superman, but he forgets he's human. I've always respected his hustle and dedication, but everybody has a breaking point.

Glancing down at the paper again, I can't help but feel a nudge in my gut that I don't quite understand. "So you think I'd be good for this? I've never been much for leadership."

I didn't even know any coaching positions were still being looked for. And the thought of me helping the new players...Well, it would put me back on the field. But how would I feel not being one of the guys on it?

Caleb nods. "You know the same things I do, and you said yourself the current coach is a joke. What better way to change that than to be the change the team needs? You're in grad school too. You'd be just as well off getting the financial help. Plus, if you're on staff, then maybe things with you and Rachel won't seem so damning."

Her name perks my ears up. Normally, everyone is telling me to quit pursuing her. Not that they know the actual details of what has or hasn't happened between me and our former adviser. "You've really thought this out, huh?"

He shrugs a shoulder. "I'm looking out for a buddy. You should call them or pop by the office if you're interested. But, Matt? You'd make a great coach. This is your chance to prove that. I know how you miss that life."

I do miss it. So damn much. Having to sit and watch the games, watch the Dragons struggle through every single one, kills me. But I never considered being part of the coaching staff until now. And with Rachel…

Maybe I'm a dick for admitting it, but I do. "I have to admit, part of the fun with Rach was the chase. That got old though."

I've barely seen her since coming back from break. I don't go to her office. Don't text her. I want to do both of those things, but I know she needs space to think. To figure out what she wants. I remind myself that every time I see her across campus and step toward her before stopping myself.

I grab the paper and fold it, tucking it into my back pocket. "Thanks for this," I say, patting the paper safely tucked away. "I think I'll reach out to them this afternoon."

I glance briefly at my phone to check the time, then at the door, before turning back to Caleb. "You've probably heard this a lot from your mom, but I know your dad would be proud of you. I'll miss bugging the shit out of you on campus, but I think the move you're making is a good one. Selfless."

His tone is a little rugged when he offers me a thick "Thanks" in response. He clears his throat. "Hey. Before you go…"

I wait, seeing him shift his weight from one foot to the other. "You okay?"

"You've had a good life, right? Being adopted didn't make any big changes that you regret or anything, did it?"

I blink. "Wow. Uh…"

I wasn't expecting a question like that. Caleb is only the second person that I dropped the truth bomb on about being adopted when we got talking about my parents. Rachel was the first. I never felt like I had to divulge that information, but it was obvious that they both needed to hear it because of their own situations.

"No. All the changes I went through were good ones because of my parents. I doubt I'd say the same if I were with my biological ones, whoever they are. My dad says life has a funny way of putting us where we need to be. We may not always understand it, but we should never fight it."

His Adam's apple bobs. "Thanks. Again."

I dip my chin in acknowledgment, backing toward the front door. "Oh, by the way, DJ texted about the celebration party for Shelldon." I want to roll my eyes over his tortoise's name. "They're doing RSVPs so they know how much pizza to order. It's *Teenage Mutant Ninja Turtles* themed."

Caleb snorts and can't help but smile at the ridiculous event. Because seriously. Who plans a party for a pet tortoise? DJ does. "I still can't believe Skylar agreed to getting him a tortoise."

"The things we do for love. Am I right?"

Caleb glances down, that smile only growing bigger. He must be thinking about Raine when he says, "Right."

After I head back into the frozen tundra, I can't help but think about Rachel.

What things would *I* do for love?

CHAPTER EIGHTEEN

Rachel

I'M STILL THINKING about the meeting I had with my adviser when I walk up to my apartment door and hear an enthusiastic, "Hey, neighbor!"

Startled, I nearly drop what little is left of the caffeinated drink I bought from the coffee cart before leaving campus. The meeting had gone about as well as I'd expected. With less than two months left of the semester, my adviser finally got me to apply to three different schools to move forward with my doctoral degree after an extensive conversation about what I want for my life and future.

"So you have options," is what she told me.

And she's right. I need options. And the options she gave me cost me one hundred and fifty dollars in application fees and an extra ten dollars for a rush fee since I'm applying so late.

All the schools are in Pennsylvania except for one in New York.

Based on the petite girl with bubblegum pink hair and face piercings standing with a box in her hands, I'd say the landlord finally rented the studio apartment that's been empty for almost as long as I've lived in this building.

She lifts the box. "Do you mind opening the door for

me? It's unlocked. I wanted to keep it cracked open, but my cat kept trying to get out, and she's an indoor cat only. I don't think she'd survive two seconds outside."

She's talkative, which is already the opposite of how everybody else in the building is.

Walking over, I open the door and make sure her cat isn't going to escape. "There you go."

Her smile brightens her face. "Thanks! I'm Berlin, by the way. Like the city. My parents have this thing where they name their kids after the places we were conceived. Kind of gross if you ask me, but I like my name because it's unique."

She reminds me of Brie, who can make conversation with anybody, and it makes me feel a tiny bit lighter. "It's a pretty name. I'm Rachel. No real backstory to it. It was the only name my parents could agree on."

Berlin stands straighter. "Like from *Friends*! Did they watch that? I personally only liked Phoebe and Joey from that show because everybody else annoyed me."

"Uh…" Slowly, I shake my head. "No, they weren't really sitcom people. They watched a lot of news mostly."

Her eyebrows go up, making the diamond stud in the right one shine in the sunlight. "Oh. Well, Rachel is a pretty name too."

I glance down when a white furry face tries moving past our legs. "You should probably head in before this cutie gets out. People tend to drive like maniacs on this street, so she's definitely safer inside."

Berlin nudges her cat back inside with her foot. "Well, it was nice meeting you. We should hang out sometime so you can properly meet Bunny. That's my cat. I let my four-year-old niece name her, and she doesn't know the difference between her animals yet."

My eyes go from Bunny the cat to Berlin the nervous talker who shifts on her feet under my watchful gaze.

"This is my first apartment," she adds. "I have never lived by myself before, so this is kind of a big deal for me. Dorky, huh? It's why I got a cat, so I wouldn't feel lonely. I may have accidentally gotten kicked out of my dorm room for underage drinking, so this was a last-minute decision before the next term, which is why I'm moving in so late."

Wetting my lips, I find myself cautiously smiling at her nervous admission. I've been where she is though, minus the underage drinking and sudden eviction. There's a sense of freedom when you become independent, but it's terrifying. When Mom, Dad, and Brie helped me move into my dorm at Lindon U when I was eighteen, I bawled my eyes out when it was time for them to go. I could barely see the taillights through my tears as I waved them off.

Berlin looks younger than me, but I can tell she's way better off than I was when I was her age. It probably wouldn't be the worst idea in the world to befriend my neighbor. "Well, you moved to a good town. Lindon is a safe place, so your family doesn't have to worry."

I notice the slightest drop in her shoulders as she nods, relaxing into her spot.

"And my schedule can be pretty busy," I add with a soft smile. "But I'm sure we can figure something out one of these days. Mr. Rogers always said to be kind to your neighbors, right?"

She blinks, confusion furrowing her brows. Then she

asks the dreadful question that makes me feel way older than I am. "Who?"

Is this how my mom felt when I asked her if she knew Abraham Lincoln? It wasn't malicious. The concept of time took me a while to grasp when I was a kid, is all.

When Berlin laughs so hard she snorts, I realize she's messing with me. "You should have seen your face. I know who Mr. Rogers is. I saw the movie they made about him with Tom Hanks."

Oh God. That's worse. If Mom were still alive, she'd tell me this is karma for the time I told her I liked Miley Cyrus's rendition of *"that really old song"* by Cyndi Lauper. She wouldn't let me live that down for years whenever "Girls Just Want to Have Fun" came on the radio.

Berlin's grin softens. "Anyway, thanks for being so nice. I saw the older woman with the mean face earlier, and I think she hissed at me when I tried introducing myself. I wasn't feeling super optimistic after that."

Ah. Mrs. Flynn is known to do that. I learned the same way she did. "I wouldn't take it personally, that's just how she is. But I should head inside. If you need anything, you know where I live."

"Hey! This is totally random, but since we're going to try doing the friend thing, we should go to the football game. Or a hockey game. There's a girl named Olive in my class who's a huge hockey fan. I hear the sports games are big around here, and I think I can make a jersey look cute."

It's hard not to smile at her enthusiasm even though me at football games right now probably isn't a great idea. "Ever seen *Friday Night Lights*? Lindon is like that, except the guys are—"

"Hotter," she finishes for me with a giggle. "Oh my God! I forgot. There was a hottie with a body who stopped by earlier for you. You missed him by like ten minutes. Blond, with the kind of godlike shoulders that they write about in romances. If he's not on the football team, he should be. I think he said his name was Matt. He slipped something under your door."

Trying not to think too much about her description of him, or how accurate it is, I give her a high-pitched, "Okay."

Matt almost never dropped by my apartment unless he was with me. He'd show up at my office at Lindon or stop me sometimes in passing on campus or in town, but never came here.

I unlock my door, ready to push it in, and see what Matt left when she asks, "Is he your boyfriend?" Her curiosity turns my cautious gaze back toward her. "Because if he is, good for you. He looks like he knows how to throw a girl around a bedroom, if you know what I mean."

Fighting the blush that heats my face, I clear my throat and fidget with the door handle. "He's not. But we're…really good friends."

She must hear the hesitancy in my voice because her face softens. "Oooh. *That* kind of friend. Got it. Don't worry. We've all been friend-zoned before."

I practically choke on air. "I wasn't…" I shake my head, realizing an explanation won't really do this conversation justice.

"There's nothing to be embarrassed about," she reassures me, clearly thinking I'm in some kind of denial. "It really does happen to everybody. I get friend-zoned at least once a year. Then again, I have horrible taste in men. I'm not even sure I could consider them friends."

Berlin really is just like my sister. "Berlin," I say to try to stop. "It really isn't like that. Things with us are just complicated."

But the attempt to deter her doesn't work at all. "My dad says relationships are always complicated. Even the good ones," she reasons. Her expression pinches with thought. "Then again, he told me that when he was trying to explain why he and my mom were getting divorced."

I suppose he's not wrong. "True. But trust me on this one. Somebody can be the right kind of person for you but be in your life at the completely wrong time."

She frowns at me. "That's sad."

All I say is, "That's life."

Her shoulders drop as her cat makes another appearance. Berlin nudges her back inside with her foot. "Maybe he stopped by to profess his undying love for you. I'm a glass-half-full girly."

That's sweet. "Thanks."

"And if that's not why he stopped by," she counters, shrugging. "Then we can go to the next hockey game and watch men beat up other men on the ice and take out our anger by screaming at the refs when they make bad calls."

My eyebrows go up a little. "That's…" Nice? I go with the next best choice, "Very considerate of you, Berlin. But I've actually got a lot going on right now. I'm actually about to finish grad school, and I have to get ready to go back home."

She blinks, her frown deepening. "Damn. I make a friend and she's already leaving me. I don't suppose home is the town over?"

I shake my head sadly. "Devon, Pennsylvania. Right outside of Philly."

She responds with a sigh.

"Maybe your next neighbor," I say, swallowing the lump building in my throat from how final this decision sounds, "will be somebody you can go to games with."

My lip twitches, and I realize I may actually cry if I don't go inside.

"I'll see you later," I tell her, slipping through the door and closing it behind me while fighting off the burn of tears.

I close my eyes for a second and take a deep breath, knowing I've made my choice.

To leave Lindon.

The job.

The people.

Matt.

I look down at the piece of paper on the floor that he slid under the door.

It's a list of coaching positions.

Not just in New York.

But in Pennsylvania too.

Those damn tears become harder to fight.

Then I see the Post-it attached.

Maybe it's time for us both to be happy

CHAPTER NINETEEN

Matt

I STARE AT the email for a little while longer before turning my phone screen off. Scrubbing my tired eyes, I force a smile when my mother walks into the kitchen, looking as tired as I feel.

Her hand flies to her chest when she sees me at the table, a startled noise escaping her when she flicks the light on. "What on earth—" She sucks in a deep breath, using the counter to keep herself up. "Matty. What are you doing here in the dark? Is everything all right?"

She can always tell when something isn't right from a single look. Forgoing the coffee pot she was beelining to, she walks over and pulls out the chair across from me to sit.

Her hand stretches out to pat mine. "Talk to me, sweet boy."

The email confirmation makes everything so cemented, even if the office of administration said I had the next five days to change my mind and reverse the paperwork. But…that's not what I want.

Nerves bubble in the pit of my stomach because I don't know how she's going to react to the news. But she's going to find out one way or another, so it might as well be from me.

"Where's Dad?" I ask. He's usually up before her with at least one or two cups of coffee in him by now.

She frowns. "He's still sleeping. He was up late helping the neighbor fix his car. Matty, are you okay? You seem off."

I nod, but it seems a little forced. "I'm fine, Ma. I promise. I was hoping to talk to you and Dad, that's all."

She blinks. "Okay..." My nerves must be rubbing off on her. "Should I wake him up? This seems serious if you show up at"—she checks her watch—"seven in the morning. You hate mornings."

"No, I don't," I argue too quickly.

Mom eyes me. "Honey, you used to fight us getting up to go to school when you were younger. Remember when we wished you a happy sixteenth birthday after you woke up? You told us to shut up because it was too early."

I cringe. I instantly felt bad saying that when the words slipped out of my mouth. Thankfully, they thought it was funny. But still.

"Really," she presses, moving past that. "Do I need to go get him? You have that look about you like you're about to say something you think will upset us."

I shake my head to reassure her. "No. It's not that serious."

"Oh my God," she whispers, sitting straighter. "You got a girl pregnant. It finally happened."

Finally happened? What the hell? "I didn't get anybody pregnant. Why did you think I was going to knock somebody up?"

She unabashedly lifts a shoulder. "Your dad and I both knew you weren't exactly abstinent in high school, Matty.

I'm sure that hasn't changed any. All we could hope for is that you remembered all those health classes on condoms and safe sex."

This is not where I thought this conversation was going at all. "Nobody is pregnant, Ma."

I can see the relief in her eyes.

"I…" *Just tell her.* Sighing, my shoulders drop a fraction. "I'm dropping out of grad school."

There. It's out. Done.

I hold my breath and wait, watching her expression. But it doesn't change. "Did you hear me?"

Mom nods, a small smile curling half of her lips up at the corners. "I heard you. I'm also not surprised by the news."

What? "You're not?"

She shakes her head, patting my hand again, and sits back in her chair. "You haven't been happy since you started in the fall. I could tell your heart wasn't in it."

Huh. "You didn't say anything," I point out.

Now, her smile is full, soft, and warm. "It wasn't my place to, baby boy. You have to make your own decisions. Whatever those may be. If you continued, I would have supported you. Same if you chose to leave. I just want you to be happy."

Why did I think she'd be disappointed in me? I psyched myself up for days leading up to this conversation. I couldn't sleep last night knowing I was coming here to tell them, which is why I showed up so early to rip off the Band-Aid.

"I thought you'd be upset," I admit, feeling a little dick-ish for assuming the worst.

"I could never be upset about something that's good for

you," she says easily. "Let me ask you this. Does your decision make you feel lighter?"

I think about it. "Yes."

My shoulders aren't as tense. The weight in my chest isn't as heavy. I may not know exactly what's next, but I know I'll figure it out.

"Then this was the best choice you could have made for yourself," she tells me. "Your father and I know how sad you were to leave your friends and football behind. We could tell you were putting far more pressure on yourself than you deserved. And school was never anything you enjoyed. We were a little surprised you decided to attend anything outside of undergrad. But, like I said, that was your decision to make."

They've always been good to me. Sometimes too good. "I'm not entirely sure what I'm going to do next, but I have some ideas."

Her smile stretches. "Baby steps."

I nod, fidgeting with my hands.

"Baby steps," I repeat quietly. I stare at the scratched tabletop, tracing a face of the drawings I'd carved into it as a kid with my butter knife. "I may take a coaching position. Caleb brought it up. And…it may be good for me."

When I peek up at her, her face lightens. "I think that's a great idea. Football is in your blood. You'd be happier doing that than working in a bank passing out bills."

She's not wrong.

"I don't know if it's going to be here though," I tell her hesitantly. I was scared of telling her about dropping out as soon as I saw the email confirmation from the administration office. But telling her I may be leaving Lindon—hell, New York—was another beast. We've never been that far away from each other since they took me in. "I'm looking into a couple of positions outside of Lindon."

Interest arches her brows. "Where?"

I pause, glancing back down at the poorly drawn smiley face in the wood. "Pennsylvania," I answer quietly.

There's a long stretch of silence that has me lifting my gaze. Mom's smile remains despite the news. "Well, we're close enough to the border. And your father *has* always wanted to travel."

They would be willing to visit me? "You'd come see me even if I moved to Philly?"

The woman who I called Mom my whole life rolls her eyes at me. "Of course we would. There is nowhere you could go that we wouldn't be willing to travel the distance to in order to see you live your life. Like I said before, we want you to be happy. With your job. With your personal life. That's all a parent could ever want for their child."

I've always known that I lucked out getting them as parents, but now only solidifies it. "I love you guys," I say, swallowing down the mushy feeling rising from my chest.

"We love you too," she says, scraping her chair back. "Now I need coffee if I'm going to function the rest of the day. And while I make us some breakfast, you can tell me about the person who inspired you to go to Pennsylvania and pursue this dream. Because I have a feeling it wasn't Caleb."

I stare at her, blinking silently.

She grins knowingly over her shoulder as she grabs a pan for eggs. "A mother knows when her child is in love. And you've got it written all over that face of yours. I've been where you are before, Matty."

Love.

I lick my lips.

"I…" Rachel is at the forefront of my mind.

Mom laughs lightly. "Oh, sweetheart. There can never be any secrets between us. Just don't miss your chance if it's somebody you truly care about. I can see those wheels turning in your head. Remember what your father and I have always told you. You miss one hundred percent of the opportunities you don't take."

MY HEART IS in my ass as I knock on the door, trying to ignore the sounds of bellowing laughter followed by loud yelling from the apartment next door that sounds like girls watching a sports game based on the names they're shouting in irritation. The last time I showed up at this building, a girl with bright pink hair told me she was moving in. She didn't seem like the athletic type. Guess I was wrong. Based on the profanities at least one of them is saying to the screen, I can only assume they're throwing popcorn at.

When the door finally opens in front of me, my chest deflates with relief. I lift my arms to showcase the various blankets draped over them and the large pizza box in my hands. "I'm leaving," is the first thing I say. Cringing, I amend, "Lindon, I mean. The university. I'm done in May."

Rachel slowly drops her eyes down to examine everything I'm holding before lifting them back up to study my face with pinched brows. "You decided to drop out?"

It's not a judgmental question, but I still feel a twinge of embarrassment admitting it to her. Part of me feels like I should stick out my degree regardless of how I feel about school. If nothing else, to prove I can.

"It's not what I wanted," I tell her quietly.

There's a moment where Rachel doesn't answer but goes back to looking at the items I'm carrying like she's trying to fathom a response. Then, she says, "You want to coach."

I nod once. "I want a lot of things. Coaching is only one of them."

We stare at one another.

Her throat bobs as she looks away, the eye contact too much for her. "Matt…"

"Do you trust me?" I gently ask her, getting those pretty hazel-green eyes to lift back up from the blanket that she's transfixed on.

Her tongue slowly drags across her bottom lip as she releases a breath. "What is this about?"

"Do." I take a step closer. "You." My shoes touch the tips of her bare feet. "Trust." She looks up, and we lock eyes. "Me?"

Her nostrils flare, and then a loud sound from next door has her turning her attention to the new neighbor. "Trust doesn't matter right now, Matt. You shouldn't be here."

I don't back down. "You mean a lot to me, Rachel. You always have. Maybe it wasn't as intense back when we first met, but the more I've gotten to know you, the more I grew to like you. You're beautiful, and kind, and smart. And I get it. This is risky. Right now, it's not the right time. But in less than two months, I won't be a student at Lindon anymore."

The fact has her swallowing and shifting on her feet.

"I haven't pushed," I continue. "I haven't pressured you. I've simply been there. I watched you go on dates. Watched you grieve your mother. Watched you rebuild a relationship with your father. I've been there every step of the way because I've *wanted* to be."

She knows I have. It's nothing I need to point out, but she needs to understand that I don't do that with just anybody. Only those I truly care about.

"Watching you date those jackasses…" My eye twitches thinking about them. "I hated every second of it. But sometimes you have to do things you don't like for the people you…" My words fade because I can't say the words I've never spoken to anybody outside of my close friends and family.

"For the people you what?" she asks in a tone nothing more than a whisper.

Her question is dumbfounding to me. "Do you really need me to spell it out for you? After all this time?" When she says nothing, I chuckle lightly. "There are people who would do anything for you simply because they want to. Not because they need to. It's no different than my parents. They chose me because they *wanted* me in their lives.

"Like I said. You're beautiful, Rachel, and I've always loved knowing that I got a reaction out of you—that you allowed me to be around you for as long as I have. You haven't gotten sick of me. You always dished it back. If it were just about looks, I wouldn't have been waiting all these years, getting to know you, letting you control this situation.

I don't know how else to show you how much I..."

God. That four-letter word gets stuck in my throat. Not because I don't believe it's how I feel, but because I don't want to scare her.

But she knows.

She can see it on the tip of my tongue.

Maybe even sense it.

"Sex doesn't equal love, Matt," Rachel reasons. "You can't just teach or expect somebody to feel that way, especially not when we can't be honest with the rest of the world. Love is a feeling that overpowers everything else. Logic. Reason. Fear."

Maybe she's right. But that doesn't mean what this is isn't love or something close. "Can you honestly look me in the eye right now and say you don't have that feeling at all? That you don't feel *something*? Because we left reason behind a long damn time ago, Rachel. We keep leaving it behind, and that's got to mean something to you. It means something to me."

She wets her lips, clearly struggling for the right words. "You're a student," is the only intelligent thing she can come up with.

"Not for much longer."

Her eyes roam over my face, fear in her expression that I understand.

"Whether you like it or not, one thing is true. I don't have to teach you to love me, Rachel," I conclude. "Because you've been doing that for a long time already. You just need to admit it to yourself one day."

Her chest rises and falls, a sharp breath releasing from

her lips as she closes her eyes. And I feel it.

That little extra thickness in the air.

The crackle and spark that connects us like an invisible string.

That's when I know.

She feels it too.

And when she opens her eyes, she doesn't tell me she loves me. But she moves aside, inviting me into her space.

Telling me I'm right.

That I matter to her too.

There's nothing but silence as I move some of her living room furniture aside and begin stacking the blankets on the floor and flattening them out, then moving her couch cushions and throw pillows down to create a makeshift bed in front of her TV.

All while she watches from the doorway where she locked us in, hugging her torso. "What is happening?" she finally asks.

I set the pizza box down in the middle of the blankets and pat the empty spot beside me. "Come here," I coax.

She walks over and slowly kneels, staring at the pizza after I open the lid. "You hate veggie lovers," she whispers.

I pick up a slice with extra olives I got specifically for her and set it on a napkin. "But you don't."

The girl beside me drops her gaze back down to the food with a slight curl to her lips and an even smaller laugh under her breath. "That," she remarks, more to herself than me. "You're always doing things like that. Being nice to me. Doing things for me. Knowing me better than most people do. Even when I tried opening up to the possibility of somebody else, nobody ever compared to…" *You.*

I don't give her a flirty remark to ruin the moment, no matter the ego stroke I just got from her admission.

Her teeth dig into her bottom lip. "I've been on dates before with men who wouldn't be able to get my coffee order right even if I ordered it three times in front of them."

"Well, they're clearly idiots for not figuring out what they had when they had it," I reply easily. How many times have I stopped those guys right outside the restaurants they were supposed to meet at because I knew they weren't good enough? Too many. And I have no regrets. If I thought they had a shot, I wouldn't have stepped in. Probably. But I knew she wouldn't look at them the same way she did me.

Her gaze flickers between the food and me, then down at the blankets I set up.

"Oh," I murmur, remembering one last thing I brought over. I dig it out from my hoodie pocket that I left on the floor beside us and hold it up. "If I have nightmares tonight from those damn flying monkeys, don't judge me."

She gawks at the special edition DVD of her favorite movie in my hand. "You brought *The Wizard of Oz*?"

"It's your favorite," I say with a shrug.

The way she watches me isn't the only thing that tells me something has shifted between us. I can feel it in the air. Buzzing around us. A feeling that cocoons us in our own little world in this one heated moment.

Swallowing, I nod as she gets on her knees and swings one of her legs over my lap to sit on me. Instantly, my hands go to her hips. "I didn't do this hoping for—"

She stops me with a kiss. It's a light, quick press of our

lips that jumpstarts my heart all the same. It's impossible for her not to feel what else it awakens.

Internally groaning, I take a deep breath to try to calm down. "I don't want you to regret this," I tell her, hoping to give her time to rethink whatever is happening.

"I won't."

Fingers digging into her hips, I say, "I know you say that now, but—"

"Matt," she cuts me off, pushing down on my erection with her hips until I'm groaning underneath her. "Please."

How many times have I fantasized about her begging me to fuck her like she did last time? To make her writhe underneath me with my mouth, fingers, and cock? Too many. Way too many.

And hearing that singular word breaks any barrier I have that tells me to stop this.

Please.

Please.

Please.

The word nearly breaks me, but I realize that this isn't something I can do tonight. Not because I'd regret the feeling of Rachel opening herself to me, but because I want the next time we experience each other to be without risk or regret.

"No," I tell her, fingers digging into the fleshy part of her hips again despite the hard length begging to be let out. "The next time this happens, we're going to do it right."

Her eyes begin to glaze, so she looks away to hide the oncoming tears.

I turn her chin to meet my eyes again because seeing her

vulnerability makes this that much more real. "I'm pretty sure I've been falling in love with you a little every day, Ruby Red. Have for a long time. Will only learn to love you for a long time to come if you'll let me."

I hook an arm around her waist and tug her into me for a tight hug. For a moment, she tenses in my hold. I don't know what goes through her mind before she eventually winds her arms around me to return it.

I don't know how long we stay like that or how we manage to change positions until we're lying side by side. But we spend hours that way, one of my arms hooked around her neck, and combing through her hair while half her body rests on mine while the movie that I hate but she loves plays.

It's a long time after when I hear her say, "I'm leaving too," she whispers. "I'm going back to Pennsylvania, Matt."

I'd been waiting for her to tell me that. I think I knew she'd made up her mind before she even did.

"Our story isn't over yet, Rach," I tell her, pressing a kiss against the top of her head. "It's barely beginning."

She looks up at me. "I'll be gone."

I lift a shoulder, moving hair away from her face with a soft smile. "Maybe one day I'll find myself in your neck of the woods."

Rachel only stares.

I look to her lips, then back up at her eyes.

"Yeah," I say, hugging her into me again and relishing in how warm she feels. "Our story definitely isn't over yet."

CHAPTER TWENTY

Rachel

THE SILKY ROBE goes to my shins, blowing in the slight breeze that also tries picking up the cap secured by bobby pins to my waved hair. Brie drove all the way from her house early this morning just to doll me up like her own personal Barbie. It was obvious that the one-month-old Loreli, or Rory for short, had kept her up most of the night. But she still came, baggy eyes, tired yawns, and all.

I search the stands filled with people, wondering if the adrenaline I feel on the football field is what always coursed through the Dragons' blood when they were on the turf. It's a role reversal that makes me smile.

The last six years here have been a roller-coaster ride with ups and downs I didn't know if I'd survive. Losing Mom had been the hardest part. Knowing she's not here to see me get my degree for a second time...

God. It hurt.

It really, really hurt.

But it also makes me that much happier when I see the familiar faces in the crowd: Dad, Brie, Ryan, my favorite niece, Rory, and even Tatum. And two rows over is a sixth face that makes my heart do a little dance.

Matthew.

He came.

My chest swells with a fuzzy warmth that travels through each of my limbs. I swear I see him lift a hand as if he knows I'm watching him.

I start to lift my hand, too, but stop myself when my row is called.

It's time.

My last moment at Lindon U.

I stand, eyes going to the sky.

"I wish you were here, Mom," I whisper, smiling at the clouds roaming above me.

When it's my turn, I hear a section of the stands cheering me on. Way more than from the people I counted before that were here for me.

That's when I see them.

Bea from the bakery.

Caleb.

Daniel and his girlfriend Skylar.

Justin Brady, the former quarterback.

And at least three or four more standing beside them. They're all in red Lindon U jerseys.

Dragons.

Here to support me.

But how did they…?

Then I see what Matt is wearing.

A Jersey with a double zero on it.

You're part of the family, he'd told me once.

Emotion settles into the back of my throat.

I have both of my families here today.

And it's a bittersweet feeling knowing I'm leaving my

chosen one behind.

Matt points to his jersey, and I know he's smiling. And I can't help but smile back, even if he can't see me.

✪

BERLIN FOLDS A pair of jeans and sets them in my suitcase. "I can't believe you're leaving. Who is going to drink wine with me, help dye my hair, and go to sports games?"

I look at her lavender hair, which didn't turn out nearly as bad as I worried it would when she pushed the box of dye in my hands last night.

"Olive," I answer easily. "I heard you two yelling at the TV again last night. What were you watching?"

She tucks her legs under her. "The Rangers game. If you thought college hockey was violent, you should watch a pro game."

I push past the sadness that has reddened my eyes since turning in my resignation this morning and smile at her. "You're turning into a real fan, aren't you? I heard some of the stuff you were shouting. Olive has been teaching you the proper terms."

Berlin grabs another article from my bed and starts folding it. "Yes. No more calling the puck a hockey ball or telling her I think the players that they look hot in their costumes."

I pause what I'm doing. "Costumes?"

She shrugs. "I only did it once...or three times. Whatever. They do look good in them though."

I can't help but laugh. "I'm glad you have Olive," I tell her, grabbing her hand and squeezing it. "And I'm going to miss you. Thank you for helping me pack. I didn't think I acquired this much stuff."

She slides off the bed and walks over to where I'm tucking things into a box, picking up a picture of Brie and me. "Are you sure this is your only option?"

"It's the option that makes sense."

Turning, I wrap the frame in an old tee and carefully put it into the box with my other belongings. Dad hired a moving truck to come get my things and bring them back to Pennsylvania after I told them they didn't need to come all this way to help me.

Sitting on the edge of my bed, I frown at the mess scattered everywhere. Boxes are stacked along the walls, clothes are thrown over different pieces of furniture, and fast-food containers, a la Berlin, are on every surface.

"Did you hear back from the high school?" she asks, leaning against the dresser.

Devon Central School, the very same district my mother used to work at, was excited about my interest in a substitution position but offered me a part-time guidance counselor position after learning about the work I did with the players on the football team. The online interview seemed to go well, especially when they told me they would be "honored to have somebody with the same spirit as Lorilei Holloway" back in their halls.

Until I could save up to find a better apartment nearby, I was willing to accept it and work my way up until a full-time position or something better suited for me in the future.

"They called me this morning," I reply. "I start training in a few weeks but won't start officially until after summer.

It'll give me some time to settle in."

She genuinely looks happy for me. "I'm glad things are lining up for you, even if you're ditching me."

I smile at her. "You'll be fine."

The raspberry she blows out says otherwise.

A knock on the door has both of us turning in confusion. "Did you invite Olive over?"

Berlin shakes her head. "No. She's hanging out with Skylar and Sky's boyfriend, DJ, tonight. They're at some book club discussing fairy porn or something."

I walk to the door and peek out the curtain, staring wide-eyed at the person standing behind the glass. "Oh my God."

"What?"

Opening up, I don't get a word in edgewise before Matt walks in, grabs my face, and kisses me.

It's the kind of kiss that can make you forget your name, family, and passwords. More importantly, it's the kind of kiss that makes you forget your problems.

"Whoa, okay." Berlin's voice quickly has Matt backing up in startled surprise. "I'm no stranger to porn or anything, but it's different when you know the people you're watching. So before clothes start coming off, I'm going to get out of here."

She squeezes my hand, grins at Matt, and then mouths, "*get it, girl*," as she backs out my front door with both her thumbs up.

Matt's hand goes back to my cheek, surprisingly unfazed by my neighbor. "Go out with me."

I blink. "Matt, I—"

"You're leaving," he finishes. "I know."

"That's not what I was going to say," I tell him, swallowing the heartbeat rising up my throat.

"Then what were you going to say?"

My heartbeat only increases, drumming wildly until it echoes in my ears. "I was going to say that I'm not working for Lindon anymore."

Matt's eyes flash. "And I'm not a student."

I slowly shake my head. "Are you really going to apply for coaching positions in Pennsylvania?"

He dips his chin. "I already did."

I stare wide-eyed. "What?"

"I got a job," he tells me, his lips trailing up my jaw and to my ear. "At a college in Pennsylvania."

He nips the lobe of my ear, causing a breath to whistle past my lips.

"Why Pennsylvania?"

His chuckle makes warm air caress my ear. "I think you and I both know the answer to that," he murmurs, making goose bumps pebble my arms.

My hands go to his sides. "You're going to move for me?" I whisper.

What was it I'd told my sister? That I'd know if it was love if someone was willing to pack up their life for me.

His mouth makes a path from my ear over my cheek and pecks the tip of my nose. Every single place those kisses go builds the fire throughout my veins. "You were right," I tell him, his lips hovering over mine.

"About?"

My fingers curl into his shirt. "You didn't need to teach me how to love you. It just…happened. Before I could even stop it. Before I ever had the chance to."

I can't describe the sound that comes from him, but suddenly he kicks the door closed with his foot and smashes his lips against mine. It's hot and heated and needy as he guides me backward until I hit the wall. He pins me against it with his hips until I feel the hardness pressing against my softest spot, causing me to groan into his mouth.

His fingers thread through my hair, gripping from the scalp and pulling my head back to expose my neck.

Rolling his hips, I refrain from making the same noise he got from me the first time, no matter how good he feels against me. His fingers grip my hair tighter until there's a blissful bite of pain as he guides us into the bedroom. He doesn't let go until my knees are pressed against the edge of the mattress, where he forces me to sit.

"You're going to watch me show you how much I love you," he states, unwinding his hold on my hair and cupping my chin to lock our gazes. "If you look away for even a second, I'll start over again until you're begging me to stop."

I swallow past the lump in my throat as I watch him sink to his knees. "Matt—"

He peels off my sweatpants and spreads my legs. "You're going to watch quietly," he cuts me off. "Starting now."

My lips part to protest but are quickly silenced as he gets his first taste with no hesitation. One of my hands darts to the comforter beside me, fingers digging into the soft duvet, while the other finds his head and threads into his hair.

You're going to watch me show you how much I love you.

I'm transfixed on how his face disappears between my thighs. He works me with his skillful lips and tongue, nipping and sucking and letting his fingers tease my entrance until a tingle of pleasure shoots down my spine and arches my butt from the bed.

He keeps going for what feels like forever, working ten times harder the more I try fighting off the impending orgasm that shakes my thighs positioned on either side of his head.

Matt wins.

Fingers gripping his hair as I detonate around him, I fall back onto the bed with a drawn-out moan. Sparks shoot down my legs as he works me through the quivers and quakes that wrack my body.

When I'm fully sated, I let out a long breath and stare at the ceiling. His fingers squeeze my inner thighs, catching my attention.

Rising from his knees, he grins with my arousal still on his mouth. "You looked away," he informs me, those blue-gray eyes nearly coal black with a lust that makes me a little terrified. "You know what that means."

Before I can ask, he's ripping off my shirt until I'm completely bare in front of him. "Now you get to watch me do it all again."

Little black dots burst in my eyes as he inserts two of his fingers inside me, hooking them to hit the perfect spot that crests yet another wave of pleasure through me.

Then he crawls up my body, his jeans and boxers long forgotten on the floor, and kisses me slowly, gently.

"Why?" I ask him, out of breath. I'm not even sure what I'm asking, but my brain is mush, and my body is completely in his control.

His lips go to one corner of my mouth, then the other, before ghosting over them fully and whispering, "Because I love you."

My heart reacts to those words like it's the first time I'm hearing them.

"And because I'm coming to Pennsylvania," he answers, nudging himself inside me and swallowing my gasp with his mouth when he pushes in.

I wrap my arms around his neck, pulling away slightly and staring up at him. It's hard to think straight when he fills me, hitching one of my legs over his hip.

"Matt—"

"Shh," he coaxes, kissing me again. "We have plenty of time, baby."

I moan into his mouth when he surges forward, following a rhythm that has my other leg mimicking the first to give him more access.

Our mouths battle it out as our bodies work together to create the blissful sensation that has us panting and sweaty.

He grabs my hair, pulling my head back to bite down on my neck. That's all it takes before I arch up and let go of every single thing holding me back.

Shortly after, he follows until we're nothing but tangled limbs on the bed.

It's ten, or maybe thirty, minutes later when I finally find my voice. "Your family is here in Lindon."

He hums, hugging me against his side and nuzzling his nose against the top of my head. "I guess that's true, but my new job is in Pennsylvania."

All I can do is gape at him.

Matt chuckles, tweaking my chin. "In the fall, I'll be Penn State's newest athletic adviser and be added on as an offensive coordinator after their current OC retires."

All of this has me speechless. He did this for me? For us?

"Do you know what that means?" he asks, smiling when I slowly shake my head. "It means that we're free, Rach. And there's nothing anybody can do about it."

"I'm leaving tomorrow afternoon, Matt."

His hold on my chin tightens for only a moment before he pulls me back down to him. "I guess that means we'll have to make our date count until I can join you in Pennsylvania this summer."

He's moving to a different state.

My home state.

"Are you sure this is what you want?" I press, hoping it's a choice he won't regret. "You love your mom and dad. Your friends are here."

"You said it yourself," he answers. "I thrive on the field. I'm meant to coach. By taking the position at Penn, I can still do that and help the players outside the turf. It won't even matter if I finish my master's program because I can still do what I love."

He's been on the fence about finishing his degree ever since he opted to enroll as a graduate student, but he's already put in a lot of work. "I do believe you're meant to be out there, but I'd hate for you to give up the work you've put in."

Matt makes a thoughtful noise. "You don't know why I enrolled, do you?"

My brows pinch. "You wanted a backup plan for the

future. Something practical."

He chuckles, clearly making me second-guess myself. "I wanted you. To be around you. Have reasons to see you. I could have walked away from undergrad and figured out what to do with my life, but then I wouldn't be here."

I can't believe he stayed to be near me. "We couldn't be together though."

"Life is all about timing, Rach. Even if I chose to get a job and not bother with grad school, you wouldn't have been ready for me. I know you wouldn't have. You were still processing so much with your father and Tatum and your mom. I don't think it would have mattered."

As I'm about to argue, I stop myself. Because he's right. My problems with my father and his girlfriend went beyond two people falling for each other at the worst time. It even went past their age difference. Those were factors, but not the reason why I would have held myself back.

I didn't want to be a hypocrite or let somebody in just to watch them leave again, and I certainly didn't want to have my heart broken.

So, sure. Maybe he has a point. Even if there weren't policies and consequences between us, plenty of barriers were still in place that were nearly impossible to destroy.

"If friendship was all I could get, I was going to take it until you were ready," he puts simply.

He's too good for me.

"I told you before, Ruby Red. Our story isn't over yet."

EPILOGUE
Rachel

A S I'M UNLOADING the last box into my brand-new office, there are a couple of knocks on the door.

I look behind me, unable to stop smiling, when I see Matt standing there.

He looks good in a navy blue polo shirt with Penn State on the breast pocket and one of his hands tucked into the front pocket of his khakis. He looks professional—older than his twenty-three with some slight scruff on his jaw that doesn't make him look as baby-faced.

"I said if I'm ever in town, I'd stop by…" He says with a half-grin on his face, holding up a pair of car keys. "So, how about I take you to lunch?"

I drop everything I'm doing and walk over to the boy who I've slowly fallen in love with over the past few years.

I plant the softest kiss on his lips. "I'd love that," I tell him honestly.

It's been a long summer away from one another, even though we've talked every day. He found a place not too far from Penn State or my apartment and moved in about a week ago. Brie and Ryan met him within two days, hounding him with inappropriate questions that made me blush and Matt laugh.

One day, I'm sure he'll meet my father.

When we're ready.

Until then… "I know a place with really good Philly cheesesteaks," I tell him, knowing they're his favorite.

He kisses me again. "You read my mind, Ruby Red."

When we walk out of my office, we do it holding hands.

I don't look over my shoulder as if somebody can see me, scared of the repercussions.

We sit together at the restaurant.

We laugh.

And we plan our next official date.

EPILOGUE TWO

Matt

M Y HANDS ARE clammy. When was the last time my palms were this sweaty? I can't remember.

I try acting nonchalant as we wait in the waiting room. Rachel's leg bounces with nerves as she stares at the door that the doctor disappeared behind. If I touch her to calm her down, she'll probably feel how nervous I am too.

But not for the same reasons.

Rachel's hand rises to her mouth, where her front teeth bite down on her thumbnail. We've been waiting for this day for over a month, and when we were told the results were in, I knew there was no point in waiting to get them.

"You okay?" I ask softly.

Rachel turns to me, lowering her thumb with a sheepish smile. "Yes. No." She frowns. "I'm not sure."

Understandable. "It'll be okay," I promise, nudging her knee with mine. "No matter what the results are, we're in this together."

My heart starts beating ten times faster at those words that she smiles over. I can see the hesitation in her eyes as she asks, "No matter what the test results are?"

She's scared, but nothing about what the lab tests say will change my mind. "No matter what they say," I say, "we're in this together."

She reaches for my leg, squeezing just above my knee as the door opens, and we're called back.

There's no small talk. No conversation about the weather or the seasons quickly changing. They know why we're here and what we're here for, so they get down to it.

The woman who guided us into the little private room in the back hands us a folded piece of paper.

It was Brie's second baby announcement that sparked Rachel's interest in finding out if she was a carrier of Huntington's disease. There was a fifty percent chance she had the gene, and it'd taken months of back and forth for her to take the step that would finally answer her question.

The woman leaves us alone to read the results.

As Rachel stares at the paper, I kneel in front of her in the chair she occupies. "Look at me," I say gently.

Her eyes peek at me through her lashes.

I reach into the pocket of my pants and wrap my fingers around something velvet. "No matter what," I remind her, pulling the jewelry box out and revealing it to her in my palm. "We're in this together. Regardless of the results. No matter what we might have to face."

Rachel's eyes grow twice the size they were when I open the ring box to show her what's inside. It's not much, but I know the simple gold band and diamond are exactly her style. Nothing too flashy or gaudy, but classy and elegant.

"Matthew…"

"You don't have to give me an answer right now," I tell her, closing the box and setting it on her lap. "I just wanted to let you know that today doesn't change a thing for me. It never will."

I've known the girl in front of me for years. Gotten the chance to truly be with her for the past fourteen months. We see each other every day. Talk to each other every day on the off chance we can't spend the night together at one of our places, and we've talked about moving in together before our leases have to be renewed.

Her eyes become glassy as she stares at the ring and then the paper in her hand.

"Together," she repeats, opening the results.

She stares.

And stares.

And stares.

Then a puff of air releases from her parted lips as she lowers the paper.

She closes her eyes.

"Together," she says again.

If you liked TEACH YOU TO LOVE ME make sure to leave a review.

Read an excerpt of **DARE YOU TO HATE ME**
and get to know Aiden and Ivy!

CHAPTER ONE

Ivy

THE POUNDING HEADACHE in my temples matches the loud *thumping* of my housemate's headboard smacking into the wall above me. Covering my face with the stained, flattened, pillow does little to drown out what's going on upstairs. What's *always* going on. That's what you get when your rent is dirt cheap—four hours of sleep a night in a party house that I heard had a spare room through the grapevine at work.

I didn't realize when I showed up with two measly bags and the clothes on my back that I'd be shoved in the dank, musty half-finished basement that smells like old socks and lavender Febreze and brushed off with barely a second look from the six other girls I live with. Or that most of them like to party, drink, and screw, usually in that order, whenever they get the chance to.

But I'd endure. I have nowhere else to go in this godforsaken town thanks to my spontaneous decision to get my life together and have no room to judge what Sydney is currently doing in the confines of her bedroom. I've done far worse, far more times, I'm sure of it.

Groaning when I drag myself out of bed, I throw on my typical Bea's Bakery attire, blue jeans and a black long-sleeve shirt that has the business's cartoon bee logo flying around a cupcake across the chest and slide a brush through my faded blue hair. I'm lucky Beatrice Olsen, the elderly woman who owns the bakery here in Lindon, New York, hasn't asked me to dye it back to my natural color. The brown copper color my hair used to be had natural red and caramel highlights in the sunlight, a unique mixture my mother used to tell me she envied because it took a lot of money at salons to produce the same results.

No longer is my hair a mixture of my parents'—my mother's pretty copper and my father's chocolate brown. The long locks I desperately need to cut soon are one of the few things I can change about myself. It's a chance to be someone else even temporarily, an identity of my own, unattached to my past or the people I walked away from.

It's barely seven in the morning when I slip upstairs, ignoring the moans coming from the only other door off the kitchen besides mine, and focus on grabbing my Starbucks iced coffee from the fridge and leaving before my housemate and her hookup are done.

People have rarely bothered me since I moved in back in July. The large white two-story Victorian is well known around campus as the place to party. Unfortunately, that means a lot of guests stay overnight—hookups, people too drunk to drive, and the occasional significant other pop up from time to time when I'm not locked in my room.

Raine, the only girl here who acts like I don't have fleas, and her boyfriend Caleb are two people I tolerate. The few times I've been hassled by one of my roommate's hookups, it's always Caleb, the laid-back but charming running back for Lindon University's football team, who gets them to leave me alone. Since words aren't my forte, I thank him with homemade baked goods which he takes to his place that's rumored to house a handful of other football players.

I never ask for confirmation, and he never remarks on the double batch of desserts I send his way figuring there are other massive men to feed. He simply brings back the clean dishes for the next time he has to fend off some asshole who can't take no for an answer.

My shift at the local bakery is like any other when I clock in, tie a small white apron around my waist, and help Bea's granddaughter, Elena, get the pastries out for the day. There are early morning regulars, older couples who love the Sunday specials, that I get to greet and make easy conversation with, and a few grad students who don't totally piss me off when they hang around using the Wi-Fi.

In Lindon, everyone knows everyone even though the college brings in over three thousand students each semester. It's what I imagine a real-life Stars Hollow from *Gilmore Girls* would feel like if it were a small city. The customers who come in the bakery always have a new slice of gossip to share, and you're never safe from being one of the topics.

The sixteen-year-old sitting on the back counter with her legs dangling over the side in a swinging motion pokes at my hair. "When are you going to redye this?"

I make a face as I pour myself a cup of coffee since the

one I brought didn't cut it. I'll need the extra caffeine after the last hour and a half turned into a nonstop morning rush. "I don't know. I'm not sure what color I want to do next."

And I'm broke, I silently add, blowing on the steam billowing from the cup. No matter how hard I save up what little extra money Bea not-so-subtly sneaks into my paychecks each week, it's still not enough to justify buying pointless little things.

"I can do it," she offers, sipping on some disgusting concoction that only she drinks.

Setting my cup under the counter so I don't accidently spill it, I say, "I'm good, Lena."

Lena is sweet enough. A little too talkative and bubbly for my liking, especially first thing in the morning, but I've worked with worse—spoiled teenage brats and older people who are asses. My biggest problem with the social butterfly is how much she reminds me of what could have been before I messed everything up. It's not her fault that her tender age and obvious naivety triggers something dark inside of me that I prefer to bottle up.

It's something I have to deal with every time she complains about things like her mother refusing to extend her curfew, let her date, or wear certain types of clothing when she's out. Her nose always crinkles when I say, "I don't see why you're so upset. Your mother loves you, that's why she's hard on you."

Lena's about to say something when her eyes get big and she kicks me a little too hard in the back of the thigh with her favorite checkered platform Vans. "He's back!"

I know instantly who she's talking about before I even

turn to scope out the entrance. The little bell on the door goes off at the same time every Sunday, and Elena feels the need to point him, and his staring, out each week. He'll wait to order until the line is down before he gets the same thing as always—a small coffee, no cream or sugar, six milks, and half an everything bagel.

All the bagels are homemade and probably the best things I've ever eaten. Bea makes them herself, never trusting anybody else to get them right. She stays late, makes the dough, bakes them, and leaves them for us to heat whenever they're ordered the following day. They sell out every time.

The only reason I don't raise a fit about the not-so-mystery-man's order is because I get to eat the other half since nobody in their right mind would only order half of the delicious doughy treat.

I manage to roll my eyes without the person I'm cashing out seeing. "Calm down. And no kicking. Your excitement gives me bruises."

She scoffs behind me, and I'm sure if I glance over my shoulder I'll see her arms crossed and her pink glossy lips sticking out in a pout. Sure enough, when I steal a look, she's doing just that. "It's not hard to make you bruise when you're barely a shade darker than white."

I grin to myself and pass the man his change, coffee, and bag of pastries, before turning to her. "Whatever. And he's just another customer, so chill."

Now *she* rolls her eyes, disbelief coated in them like they always are when I brush off the appearance of Lindon U's star tight end. He's a guy who excels at what he does, I'll give him that. But he's still *just* a guy—a guy who orders half a bagel like some kind of carb-hating demon while still paying full price for it.

"He's coming over," she squeaks, cheeks turning red like they always do in his presence. It's why, as much as I want to pass him off to her to avoid any conversation, I have to handle it so she doesn't make a fool of herself.

I know some of the guys on Lindon's U football team from my intro classes this semester, making it easier to handle the mostly overbearing team members better than some when they come in. Biological Anthropology is where a lot of athletes wind up because of the professor's reputation for giving out easy A's. I guess it makes sense that sports teams would flock to classes like that since their GPA is required to be over a 2.5 to stay on any team here, but their presence makes it harder to concentrate. They're all stupidly attractive and considering their cocky smiles and flirty winks at the females (and males) who notice, they know they are too.

I've seen some of the players use the attention to their advantage, making me scoff every single time they convince some poor victim to help them with homework, papers, or buy them something here at Bea's.

Maybe if I were any other person, with any other experi-ence, I'd succumb to their looks as well—give them free things when they approach me at the counter, agree to study and wind up with my shirt up and jeans down in the stacks at the library or pinned between a wall and bulky body in the locker room. Attractive people make you do stupid things out of human need, but it's the ones who have the whole package that are the most dangerous.

Especially the one stopping in front of the cash register right now.

According to ESPN, the man towering over my five-nine stature is close to six-six. Tall. Powerful. Authoritative. I'll never forget the day he walked into Bea's with his normal group of friends all bellowing over something stupid. His head was down, his shoulders hunched, his hands stuffed into the pockets of his red Lindon U sweatshirt like he didn't want anybody to bother him, but somehow I knew.

I knew I'd be met with electric blue eyes when he looked up—the kind impossible not to be enamored with. And if I looked close enough, I'd see a formation of freckles on the right side of his face that resembles the big dipper.

What I didn't expect was how defined his jaw became, slightly squared and clean of any scruff most of the time, a patrician nose free from any breaks despite his aggressive sport, and a set of lips that are enviously fuller than mine.

He's the perfect type of football player in my eyes. Tanner from the summer sun, built but not overly so despite all the training he does, and a smile that's so white I hear Crest reached out to him on his Instagram to be featured. Whether that's true or not, I don't know. I don't have social media these days, just housemates who love to gossip. Especially about the football players who have made a splash on ESPN and local news stations with talks of going pro.

"Your usual?" I greet him, careful to keep my tone even despite the way my skin tingles as he towers over the register.

One of his brows, dark brown like the hair on his head, quirks. "Am I that predictable?"

It's Elena who chirps out a "Yep."

He chuckles, swiping one of those huge hands through the tresses of thick hair that are longer on the top versus the sides. "The usual then."

I try not to focus on the low, husky tone of his voice that causes bumps to rise over my arms. He's twenty-one, but he doesn't sound it. Before I settled for a half-renovated basement, I couch-surfed with strangers. Most of them who were men older than my twenty years with every intention of making me pay them in some way, and usually not with money.

Aiden Griffith doesn't give me the same vibes those guys do, though. I've had limited interactions with him since the day he walked in and stared in my direction until every inch of me felt the lick of flames from his burning blue gaze. He'll order, I'll tell him it's ready, and he'll give me a generic "have a good day" knowing I'll never offer an opportunity for more. One time he told me my shoe was untied, which I'd already figured out after almost falling on my face with a tray full of breakfast for table three—who happened to be his buddies. Most of them besides Caleb and DJ, a guy from my anthropology class, laughed at my clumsiness until Aiden shot them a look. They shut up quickly.

It makes no sense to me why a player so sought-after would be at a school like Lindon. We're not division one. If anything, we're the misfit college—once thriving, now barely making ends meet if not for the championships the football team wins. I've heard people say that athletes who blow it at other schools come here to redeem themselves. Some of them make a future for themselves in the pros after their second chance, and others fizzle out.

I wonder which the man in front of me is.

I've been to a few games in the last year when I was squatting near campus and checking out my financial options for enrollment. Thanks to having nothing to my name, and a decent GED score, financial aid pulled through for me when I was accepted. I know a little bit about the game, but not what each position is called or what the scoring system is like. Most of what I do understand comes from the sixteen-year-old I work with who feels the need to read out sports stats from online that are more like code to me than English. But because I want to understand, to learn after he walked in the first time, I try piecing together the little tidbits she always babbles about. Who's the best, who's going pro, who won't get the chance—Lena and her grandmother have predictions for the entire team, and like most of Lindon, they're in agreement that Aiden Griffith can make it to the top.

Elena is the conversationalist in this transaction as I prepare Aiden's coffee because my tongue is too heavy. "Grandma Bea said the Dragons are going to kick butt all the way to the championships."

From the corner of my eye, I see the tight end's lips twitch upward, like he doesn't want to be cocky but can't pretend it's untrue. "That's the plan. Are you coming to support us?"

According to some of the locals that come in for coffee, the university has broken the records for most wins at home and away because of the team they've had the last two years.

"Are you kidding? I wouldn't miss it! Bea was going to shut down early until Ivyprofen here said she'd stay and close." Lena snorts while I roll my eyes at her nickname for me. "I don't know why. Nobody will be here except her."

A new set of eyes focuses on my face, but I busy myself by spreading the olive oil and sea salt butter he likes over his bagel. "Ivyprofen?" There's amusement in his tone, but he doesn't let either of us explain that Elena calls me that because she says I'm a pain and she needs medicine after dealing with me. Instead, he proceeds to ask, "Not a fan of football, huh?"

All I give him is a stiff shrug, and even the smallest upward movement feels draining. I know better than to believe it's from exhaustion, but refuse to acknowledge the real reason behind the tightness consuming my body.

I remind myself I'm here to work, not make conversation with every customer that comes in. Especially not him.

As Elena goes to answer for me, her grandmother walks out from the back. "Lena, I need you to help me take out the bins of dough from the back and set them in the kitchen for me. We have a lot of baking to do today for the week."

I usually help with the week's preparations, but Elena expressed interest in learning her grandmother's recipes, so I took a step back. I want to believe Bea, or Bets as I call her, sees me as another grandchild—one of the twelve she lays claim to. But I know I'm not, and that I shouldn't try so hard to be.

You're here for a paycheck, I tell myself again silently. *Not a family.*

Feeling my throat close up as I wrap up the bagel and stick it into a bag, I begin folding the top to complete the order when I hear, "Ivy."

It's not a roll off the tongue like he's testing its sound.

It's in familiarity.

You're here for a paycheck, I tell myself once more as I turn on my heels and pass him the white bag and coffee cup without meeting those bright blue eyes. "That'll be $4.25 please."

"Ivy," he repeats, and I wonder if he can hear how hard my heart thumps with the sound of my name coming from his lips again.

"Cash or credit?" I press, staring at the machine's buttons, ignoring the pumping organ in my chest.

"Iv—"

"We also take Dragon Dollars," I cut him off, gesturing toward the new promotion. Any college student that comes in can pay by scanning their student I.D card.

He cusses under his breath. "You're just going to keep pretending then?" Even though his words are barely more than a hushed murmur under his breath, I feel them deeper than that. They sweep under my skin and squeeze my heart until I hear it *crack* from the pressure.

All I give him is, "Yes."

Because pretending is all I can do to get through today without remembering the past or the girl who confided in a boy before he left her to her demons four years ago.

I don't blame Aiden.

And I've never forgotten him either.

That's the problem.

Read it today

ACKNOWLEDGMENTS

I am so grateful to those who have stuck with me as I (very slowly) get the Lindon U series out. I know it's been a long journey since DARE YOU TO HATE ME released back in 2021. The fact you've followed along and read each character's stories means the world to me.

To my cover designer Letitia Hasser, you always make such stunning covers! And to Marla at Proofing Style, thank you for polishing my newest book baby.

I also want to shout out my best friend Jessica who listened to me stress about Matt and Rachel for the better part of two years. I've written three different versions of their story and was never happy with it until this draft. You heard the journey and I'm grateful you listen to me ranty voice messages every day.

Thank you for continuing to read my books!

Until next time,
B

ABOUT THE AUTHOR

B. Celeste is a new adult and contemporary romance author who gives voices to raw, realistic characters with emotional storylines that tug on the heartstrings. She was born and raised in upstate New York, where she still resides with her four-legged feline sidekick, Oliver "Ollie" Queen. Her love for reading and writing began at an early age and only grew stronger after getting a BA in English and an MFA in English and creative writing. When she's not writing, she's working out, binge-watching reality game shows, and spending time with her friends and family.

Website:
authorbceleste.com

Facebook:
AuthorBCeleste

Instagram:
@authorbceleste

TikTok:
@authorbceleste